THE BLACKSMITH'S MAIL ORDER DOCTOR

IRON CREEK BRIDES, BOOK TWO

KARLA GRACEY

© 2021 by Karla Gracey

All Rights Reserved. No part of this publication may be copied, reproduced in any format, by any means, electronic or otherwise, without prior consent from the copyright owner and publisher of this book.

This is a work of fiction. Names, characters, businesses, places, events and incidents are either the products of the author's imagination or used in a fictitious manner. Any resemblance to actual persons, living or dead, or actual events, or places is purely coincidental.

This book is dedicated to all of my faithful readers, without whom I would be nothing. I thank you for the support, reviews, love, and friendship you have shown me as we have gone through this journey together. I am truly blessed to have such a wonderful readership.

CHARACTER LIST

- **Alec Jenks – blacksmith.**
- **Anna Macdonald – doctor.**
- Albert Brennan – law student/lawyer whose intention in studying law and in his practice of it is to help women and others often let down by the justice system
- Mrs. Phelps – Anna's landlady in Boston
- Aunt Lilah – Alec's aunt in Chicago
- Mrs. Emmeline Jenks – Alec's mother.
- Dr. Cornelius Jenks – Alec's deceased father
- Dr. Skallin – Anna's mentor and long-time supporter
- Dr. Andrew Lancelot – doctor, retiring from practice in Iron Creek.
- Derek Thompson – hotel owner in South Dakota.

- Garrett Harding – sheep farmer, lives out of town
- Katy Harding – Garrett's wife
- Jacob (Junior) Harding – Katy's son from her first husband, but very much Garrett's child
- May, Daisy, and Thomas – the Harding's triplets
- Mrs. Havermeier – boarding house owner in Chicago
- Hank Wilson – Iron Creek's postmaster
- Judd Barclay – owner of the general store
- Mary and Hector Jellicoe and their children Samuel and Thomas – Hector runs the local paper.
- Nelson Gustavson – half Ojibwe, half Swedish stagecoach driver
- The dean (Harvard) – weaselly man who doesn't want women to attend medical school
- Father Paul – Roman Catholic priest from Grand Marais who comes to Iron Creek to say Mass from time to time
- Nelly Graham – Dr. Lancelot's long-suffering nurse and secretary
- Matt Hanson – Iron Creek's sheriff
- Nathaniel Holden – pneumonia sufferer
- Zaagasikwe (Zaaga) – Garrett's Ojibwe adoptive mother
- Aandeg – Garrett's adoptive grandfather
- Wilfred, the dog

PROLOGUE

*M**ay 1872, Harvard University Medical School, Massachusetts***

The setting was almost overwhelming. No doubt, it had been designed to be so. The wood-paneled office was a place where few women had probably ever stood—other than to clean it. But Anna Macdonald was not there to clean. She was determined not to be dismissed. She straightened her spine and sat upright and proud in the hard-backed chair that was lower than that of her interviewer's and gave the small man sitting behind the large oak desk in front of her a hard stare. He shook his head as if he could hardly believe he had to explain anything of import to her. It was quite clear he expected her to accept whatever nonsense excuse he was prepared to give and leave quietly, without a fuss.

"As you can see from my file, I am an excellent student,

dedicated and driven," she said firmly. "I only ask for the opportunities this university has offered to my classmates, many of whom do not possess the qualifications and passion for medicine that I do."

"I'm sorry, Miss Macdonald, but I can't just offer you a place," the Dean said, rolling his eyes. "It simply isn't a matter of just your grades or even your tutors' recommendations. There are many factors taken into consideration when we offer a place to study medicine here."

Now it was Anna's turn to roll her eyes. He was so clearly lying to her, and he knew that she knew it. He fidgeted nervously, playing with his slightly graying shirt collar, his eyes looking anywhere but at her. He was a small weasel of a man, clad in an ill-fitting black suit with a black cravat and gold pocket watch, greasy hair, and half-moon spectacles. Anna had disliked him from the first before he'd even uttered a word in his grating, nasal whine.

"If I make an exception for you, then before you know it, every woman will want to attend classes. And then where will we be?"

"A place where everyone can come to learn who has the aptitude?" Anna suggested, arching an eyebrow at his ridiculous argument. She'd heard it a hundred times or more. Women were expected to be wives and mothers, not doctors or lawyers. They should be quiet and docile and have just enough education to bring up children but not so much that they might challenge their husband's fragile ego.

"Harvard is the finest institution in America. We can't let just anyone in," the Dean argued.

"I am well aware of that, but you can see from my school records that I am not just anyone. I have the highest grades in my class—in every subject—and three young men with lower grades than my own have already been offered places here at Harvard, in *your* medical school." From the brief look of pride upon the miserable man's face, he had noticed her stress upon the word *your*. Anna smiled inwardly and pushed onwards. "I am not asking for special treatment, sir. I wish to become a doctor. I have worked just as hard as anyone else to achieve the standards required and deserve the opportunity as much as any lesser qualified male candidate."

"But what will happen when you marry and have children?" the Dean asked, peering at her from over the top of his spectacles. "If I give you a place and you suddenly up and leave, a bright young man somewhere has had to go without his chance. A chance that is much more likely to come to full fruition, I might add."

Anna bristled at his assumption that, as a woman, she would be more likely to give up if things got tough or for some other reason. "I have no intention of quitting, sir," she insisted with the confidence of youth and the fire of injustice burning within. "And if a husband expects me to stay at home to cook and clean and raise his babies, well, then I would rather not marry at all."

The Dean tutted loudly and shook his head dismissively as

if she didn't know what she was talking about. It infuriated Anna when men did that. She understood that being a young woman made her automatically someone easily dismissed as frivolous and silly, but there were silly and frivolous men, too, and nobody ever dismissed them in this way. They were given opportunities that a woman, no matter how smart and committed, could only dream of.

"Miss Macdonald, I shall not be swayed. If I give you a place, then I have to give every woman a place. Then what happens when these women enter into marriage? Training as a physician takes many years. There are many chances for a woman to change her mind about her choice to attend or to wed and have children. If I start offering places willy-nilly to girls such as you, then America will not have sufficient doctors. That's what will happen."

Anna sighed. "How many women have applied to study medicine this year?" she asked innocently.

"Well…" The Dean blustered, rustling the papers before him as if he wished to look important and busy and to imply that she was wasting his time. "I don't see that such a question is relevant, and it is certainly none of your business."

"I think it is very relevant, given that your objection to my attending is that every young woman will want a place if you give me one. I don't need names. Just an estimate will do."

"Well, I…" he trailed off and looked at her sternly, barely concealing his seething annoyance.

"It was just me, was it not?"

"That makes little difference," he said, answering her without saying it in words.

"Oh, I think it does. If every woman wished to be here, surely they would, like me, have made an application. If they truly wanted to attend as much as I do, knowing the commitment it will take to achieve that goal, they would also have come and hounded you when that application was unsuccessful, and they realized that others with similar or lesser qualifications had been granted a place in the course, would they not?"

The Dean knew he was beaten, but Anna could take little pleasure in it. She might have won the argument, but it did not mean he would let her join the program. She needed him to let her in, and she had found that outarguing any man, especially one like this silly little prude, didn't bode well for her. Having facts and reason on her side did not seem to win her many friends.

"I will ensure you are placed upon the list of alternates," the Dean said with a heavy sigh. "You will be considered should anyone not take up their place." He avoided her gaze and quickly scribbled a letter saying as much. "I can do no more than that this year, but I will ensure that your application is reconsidered next year, should that be necessary."

"Thank you," Anna said with a soft smile. She took the letter and left his office. She had won as much as she had ever been likely to, but it was not enough. She needed an actual place, not a mythical one that could all too easily be taken away from her without her ever knowing. She knew well that if a young man was on the waiting list with her, no matter what his qualifications might be, he would be offered the chance ahead of her. It was simply the way the world worked.

Anna had to fight every step of the way. She did not wish to be difficult; she had always tried so hard to fit in and to be the kind of young woman that her parents wanted her to be— the kind of woman who might be happy merely to be a wife and mother. But she had such curiosity and such a desire to help others. Try as she might, Anna could not imagine a life where she was unable to pursue her academic goals or one where she had to give up her sense of who she was to fit in.

She had made her way out of the imposing building that housed the medical school and was walking slowly along the tree-lined paths that crisscrossed the grounds toward the street when she heard a young man's voice calling her name. "Miss Macdonald?" Anna stopped and turned to see a tall and rather gangly youth hurtling toward her. His dark gray suit jacket flapped behind him, his face was flushed, and his hair was disheveled. "It is Miss Macdonald, is it not?" he asked when he caught up to her, bending over slightly to catch his breath.

Anna nodded. "It is."

"I'm sorry, I shouldn't have been listening, but I was waiting to see the Dean myself, just out in the corridor, and I heard every word, I'm afraid. You were magnificent, if I might add." Anna smiled at the flattery, but she knew that wasn't the reason why this young man had chased her across campus.

She waited for him to catch his breath and elaborate further on his purpose in running after her.

He grinned at her and exhaled loudly before he spoke again. "You see, I came here to decline my place," he explained. "I have no desire to be a doctor at all, and though it will probably mean my father will never speak to me again, I have enrolled in the law program instead. If you want to be sure of that place you so desperately want, why don't you come with me, and I can insist that the Dean offer you the place he promised."

"Why would you do that for me?" Anna asked, touched by his sense of fairness but a little skeptical that a stranger would be so intent upon seeing her achieve what was right.

"Because I wish to study law for just such purposes," he said. "My mother is far cleverer than my father, but she had to give up any hope of a career of her own. Though she has done her best to be a good wife and mother, it is easy to see that she has been bored out of her mind. Women should have the opportunity to be whatever they wish to be. Do we not live in a modern world?"

Anna grinned. She liked this young man immensely. His ruddy cheeks and disheveled curls made him look like an overgrown cherub, but he was as fiercely passionate about his intentions as she was. She held out her hand, and he shook it. "I am delighted to meet you, Mr...?"

"Albert Brennan," he said with a grin.

"I have just one question. Why do you think the Dean

might listen to your request?" she asked him as he offered her his arm and escorted her back toward the dean's office.

"Well, that would be because my father is one of the wealthiest men in Boston and donates a very generous amount to the university every year," Mr. Brennan explained. "I don't think there will be any problem in securing you the place that you so clearly deserve." He beamed, and Anna felt her heart lift. Providence had surely smiled upon her by sending her this delightful young man.

But once they were back in the Dean's office, he did not need to rely upon his family name to support his argument. On the contrary, he showed just what a formidable courtroom advocate he would one day become. Anna left Harvard that day with a dear friend, a place to study medicine, and a future she had hardly dared hope might be hers.

January 1876, Grand Marais, Minnesota

Everyone else had left long ago, but two figures remained at the gravesite long after the service was done: a tiny, old woman clinging tightly to the arm of the huge bear of a man at her side. The gravediggers waited patiently for them to finish saying their goodbyes, occasionally adjusting their caps to fend off the intermittent rain. They didn't need to hurry them. It was right that the family of the dead pay their respects however they wished.

Alec Jenks stood quietly, staring down at the wooden coffin that lay in the grave. His broad shoulders were hunched, and one hand was thrust into the pocket of his thick woolen jacket while the other remained crooked so his mother could hold on as tightly as she wished. He glanced at her and felt his heart tear itself into pieces. She was clad all in black, with a heavy veil covering her face so nobody would know how his father's death had ravaged her and left her bare. Her clothes hung off her tiny frame. There had been no time for the seamstress to take them in. She reached into her handbag for a handkerchief and lifted her veil just enough to slip her hand inside and wipe her eyes and nose. She placed the handkerchief back where it had come from, stood up as tall as her five-foot frame allowed, exhaled loudly, and turned to Alec. "Shall we go, son?"

"Yes, Mama," he said, putting an arm around her tiny shoulders. He had towered over her since he was ten, but though she was tiny, his mother was a formidable woman; at least she had been until now. Now she was a shadow of the woman he remembered. The death of his dear papa had hit her hard. She'd become thin and frail over the past months, which was no surprise to him, given that she had barely eaten since Papa had fallen sick with consumption. Alec had tried to encourage her to take care of herself, but she had not left his father's side. It had been harrowing for them both to watch his once hale and hearty papa shrink in the bed as the illness took hold and never let him go.

Now, his father was at peace. But his mother was not, and Alec did not know how to change that. She seemed rudderless without someone to take care of. She wandered around the grand house like a wraith—the very house his father had paid the local carpenter to build upon their marriage. She went through the motions of living, but her heart was not in it.

The pair walked back to the house in silence. One of his mother's neighbors had left a casserole in the oven for them to return to, and the house smelled wonderful. But Alec knew his mother would peck at it like a bird or, worse, not even serve herself any. Alec was worried about her. She seemed unable to do anything or even to think of anything other than his father's passing. He watched her as she trudged up the stairs to change into a plain dark gray dress and put an apron on. When she returned, she sat in her chair by the fireplace in the kitchen and stared at Papa's empty one.

Alec sighed heavily. He did not know what to do to bring her back. She seemed lost completely in her grief. "Mama, what can I do?" he asked, his tone desperate.

"Nothing, son, nothing," she said sadly. "Your father was my world. With him gone, I have nothing left."

"That isn't true," he protested. "You still have me."

"But you've not needed me in years. You have your blacksmith business in Iron Creek now and that nice, neat little house of yours. I don't know why you've not taken a wife yet, but I am sure you will before long."

"And if I do, there will be grandchildren that will need

you," Alec said, feeling bewildered by her lack of purpose. She had always been so vivid, so full of life, constantly encouraging him and his father to be the very best that they could be. He couldn't remember a time when she hadn't been nagging him about how much she wanted him to settle down and have babies for her to love and care for. Now she sounded as though she thought such additions to his life would only make her own seem lonelier and bleaker.

"No, their mother will be enough for them, as I was for you." Her tone was dreary and uncaring as if all pleasure and joy in her life had been stolen from her when Papa had taken his last breath.

She needed something to do, to have a purpose once more. She had always thrived on taking care of him and his father. The solution was simple, as solutions so often are. She needed to be needed, and he could help with that. "That is not true," he said firmly. "And why do you say that you think I don't need you? I do. The blacksmith's is so busy I barely get time to feed myself, much less keep the house clean and tidy."

His mother gave him a strange look. He wasn't sure if it was of disbelief or hope, but he pressed on. "Mama, why don't you come and stay with me in Iron Creek for a while? After all this time off, I'm going to be working all hours. I need someone to take care of the day-to-day things for me. Would you do that? I can't think of anyone I'd trust more with my home and my affairs."

His mother looked up at him, her eyes filled with tears. "You want me?" she asked plaintively.

"Always," he assured her as he rushed to her side and embraced her tightly. "Mama, you have a home with me for as long as you want one."

CHAPTER 1

*A*ugust *1879, Iron Creek, Minnesota*

The sound of hammer against hot metal had always given Alec a thrill. His family had been surprised when he had announced, after yet another sneaky visit to the local forge, that he wished to leave his expensive education behind and become a blacksmith. His mother had been furious. She had thrown his privileges in his face, reminding him that she and his father had slaved to give him the finer things in life. On his mother's side of the family, his great-grandfather had been a mere laborer, his grandfather had become a master carpenter despite his humble origins, and Mama had married a doctor. Every generation had bettered itself—until him.

By comparison, his father, Dr. Cornelius Jenks, came from a long line of doctors and lawyers. It had been expected that

Alec would follow in their footsteps. His place at Yale was almost guaranteed, no matter how well or poorly he applied himself to his studies. Such privilege had never sat well with him. He hated the idea of achieving anything solely because of who he was rather than what he was capable of. Not that he wasn't bright and curious and adept at his studies.

Everyone had been shocked when Alec had announced he wished to become an apprentice, to learn a manual trade, given the opportunities that his quick mind and his upbringing could afford him. Yet, he wanted none of that. He hated being stuck in a classroom, poring over dull texts that told him nothing about life and how to live it. He despised the pompous fools in his classes who knew the price of everything and the value of nothing.

His parents had forgiven him, eventually, and had secretly been rather proud of him when he was asked to open a forge in Iron Creek immediately after he had completed his apprenticeship. They had followed him from Chicago, where his father had built a thriving practice, and set up home in Grand Marais, the nearest large town to Iron Creek, so they could visit with him often. Chicago was hectic, always on the go, so moving to Grand Marais had been a big change for them. It had worked out well, though, and all of them had enjoyed the change of pace that living in Minnesota had brought them.

Alec's reputation for high-quality work and ingenious craftsmanship had soon spread. People came from all around for his work, often commissioning intricate and difficult pieces that other smiths would have balked at. But Alec loved the challenge of creating something functional and beautiful but also intricate and technical, so he always took on these tricky pieces to give himself a challenge.

He enjoyed the variety of the work in Iron Creek, too. In Chicago, many smiths specialized in just one or two specific items, but Alec got to try his hand at things like decorative wrought-iron work, as well as the more humdrum horseshoes and barrel hoops. That variety meant he never got bored and was always looking for new ways to work the iron and steel he used to make all manner of items for his customers. He was always learning something new, and that kept his trade exciting for him.

From the corner of his eye, Alec saw a tall figure entering his yard. He looked up briefly to see it was Garrett Harding. He nodded to him, then continued with his work before the metal cooled too much. He knew Garrett wouldn't mind. The two were friends, and Alec had been delighted when asked to be Garret's son's godfather at his recent baptism. The lad, like his father, benefited from his links to the local Ojibwe tribe and had also been given a naming ceremony by them, which had been very different indeed.

When he'd finished hammering, Alec quenched the iron bar and put it back into the fire before turning to grin at his friend as he stripped off his thick leather gauntlets and threw them onto his workbench. He held out a hand as giant as a bear's paw, and Garrett shook it with a warm smile. "How are you, my friend?" he asked.

"I am well," Alec replied. "Business is good. How are Katy and my godson?"

Garrett beamed with happiness at the mention of them. "They are well, thank you, and they are why I am here. Katy insists on inviting you around for supper tonight."

"Has she been speaking with my mother?" Alec asked with a wry smile. He loved his Mama, but she refused to believe he could look after himself at all if she weren't there to cook and clean for him. And she was in Chicago for two weeks because her sister was sick.

Alec had been looking forward to having his house to himself for the first time since his father's passing over three years ago, but it seemed he was not to be trusted to cook for himself. His mother seemed to have arranged some kindly neighbors into a kind of roster to provide him with a good meal every day. He had gently let most of them down, but he would gladly accept an invitation to the Harding place up the mountain. It was quiet and peaceful up there, and both Garrett and Katy were more than happy to sit quietly and read after dinner rather than insist on endless conversation, leaving him to play with Jacob or put the lad to bed with a story.

"I can't deny that Mrs. Jenks did indeed pay us a visit before she left to visit her sister, but we would have invited you anyway. You know that."

"I do. Thank you, I would be delighted—especially if Katy is making her chicken and leek pie again."

"I shall tell her you requested it," Garrett said, tipping his hat and making to leave. "Tonight, at half-past six? I know Jacob will wish to have some time with you before his bedtime."

"I shall be there."

Alec watched his friend leave, smiling. Not so long ago, Garrett had been a confirmed bachelor and a real loner. Now he was wed with a young son he doted upon. He'd built a fine cabin to replace the old shack he had called home and had started trading again to supplement the family's income from their sheep herd, working with his Ojibwe kin. He seemed about as happy as a man could be. Alec couldn't help feeling a tiny stab of jealousy. But such a life was unlikely to be for him.

He'd made his mother a promise that she had a home with him for as long as she needed one, and she showed no signs of wanting to strike out alone. He loved her and was grateful to her for the care she took of his home—and of him—but it was stifling having her there, watching over his every movement. She wanted to be with him all the time. He had been forced to insist that she no longer stop by the forge while he was working, as it was too dangerous a place for her to be. But as soon as he left work, she was there with her eagle-eyes, watching his every move, wanting to know everything that had happened to him that day.

She'd left for Chicago four days ago, and they had already been some of the happiest Alec could remember since before his father became sick. The freedom he'd not entirely realized he'd lost was now back, and he was reveling in it. Of course, his mother had left him strict instructions, which he was ignoring, and rallied the entire town to take care of him in her absence, which he was politely declining. Having the house to himself was liberating and delightful in many ways, yet there was a nagging doubt that such solitude wouldn't always make him so happy. And as he thought about Garrett with his new wife and son, he knew what it was he longed for—not an overbearing mother, but a wife and family.

He knew no one that his mother might approve of, and he knew even fewer women who would wish to share their home with someone as interfering as Mama. But he could never ask her to leave. He had promised her a home, and he would not break that vow or any other. A bride who might be happy with that and that his mother might like would not be easy to find. Few brides would be happy to let Mama continue to run the home while being endlessly polite and always deferring to her.

Besides, Alec would not want such a woman as his bride. He longed for a wife with a bit of fire in her belly. He loved his work and at times could lose himself in it entirely, often losing all track of time until it was too dark for him to see anything but the flames of the forge. He needed a wife who could understand that kind of commitment and that his long hours didn't mean he was not just as committed to her. Most women Alec had met did not understand that his losing track of time at work was not an insult to them. And he feared that if married to him, they would end up with too little to fill their day because his mother insisted upon doing everything. They would end up waiting at home for him, feeling lonely and put upon by Mama. Such circumstances did not bode well for any relationship.

He needed the impossible. A bride with a career of her own, perhaps. Someone as dedicated to their work as he was to his own. Someone who wouldn't wish to spend too much time in the home and would be glad of someone like Mama being there to do everything required to maintain a household in her stead. It was unconventional, undoubtedly. Women were expected to stay in the home and raise their families, not to have positions that kept them away from them. He knew he was asking too much to ever expect to find someone who would fit his needs, but it didn't stop him from hoping there might be someone out there.

For once, he kept an eye on the clock as he worked that afternoon. At half-past five, he banked the fires in the forge and tidied away his tools, then headed home to have a thorough wash under the pump in the backyard. There was no jug of hot water awaiting him on the washstand with his mother gone. Somehow, she always managed to have it ready when he returned, though Alec did not know how. Perhaps she just heated up the water every half an hour or so from when she thought he might return. He shook out his head and briskly rubbed himself dry, then went inside and up the stairs. He pulled out a freshly laundered and pressed shirt from the chest at the end of his bed and pulled it over his muscular torso, quickly combed his hair, and pulled on a vest and some clean jeans, then headed up the mountain.

Jacob was on the porch, lying on a blanket and playing with his toes. He looked plump and content. He beamed and gurgled happily when Alec knelt down beside him, tickled his belly and pressed a kiss to his downy head. The creak of the screen door behind him made Alec turn round. Katy Harding smiled down at the two of them. "Good to see you, Alec," she said warmly, moving to pick up her son. She held him on one hip. "I've made your favorite, and there's enough that you can take some back with you for your lunch tomorrow."

"You're too good to me," Alec said. "And I will tell Mama that you did as you were asked and made sure I was fed."

Katy laughed. "She is a meddler, but her heart is in the right place."

"It is," Alec agreed grudgingly.

"Do you think she will ever wish to find a place of her own?"

"No," Alec said sadly. "She is the kind of woman who needs others to look after. She'd fade away without that."

Katy nodded her understanding. She kissed her baby's

cheeks and then handed him over to Alec. "Can you keep an eye on him while I finish up?"

"I'd be delighted, but do you mind if we tag along?" Alec asked cautiously. "There's something I'd like to ask you about, without Garrett being here."

"Well, if that isn't intriguing enough to make me say yes, then nothing ever will be," Katy said and laughed. "Come on in. You can put Jacob in his crib, and we can have a nice chat while I finish peeling the potatoes."

Moments later, Jacob was settled and snoozing in the crib by the vast fireplace in the kitchen. Katy reached for a bag of potatoes from the walk-in larder. It was heavy, and she struggled with it. Alec took it from her and swung it effortlessly onto the table. She grinned at him, then took a seat and picked up a knife. She began to peel the potatoes, making it look as easy as he'd made picking up the sack look. Her quick and nimble fingers made short work of the peeling, and she swept the discarded potato skins into a bucket to go out to the pig Garrett had bought to fatten up for Christmas.

"So, what do you need to talk with me about?" she asked as she worked.

"Well, Garrett told me that the two of you met because he placed an advertisement in the newspaper. I'm thinking of doing something similar, but I don't know how to go about it."

"And you feel silly asking Garrett?" Katy grinned. Men could be funny about such things.

"Something like that, but also I wanted to know why you

wrote to Garrett. There are always so many advertisements. What was it about him that drew you?"

"To tell the truth, I was desperate," Katy said. "I would have written to almost anyone who sounded like a human being with at least a hint of humility."

"Oh," Alec said. He'd rather hoped that there might be something more to it than that.

"But, of all the advertisements I did write to, Garrett's was the one I most reacted to when I saw it. He didn't talk about what he had. He talked about who he was, what he liked, and what he was looking for. I think that helped. If a woman knows that a man wants a quiet, obedient wife and she is anything but that, it is good to say that so there is no confusion later."

"I suppose that makes sense."

"So, what do you like? When you aren't in the forge, who are you? And what kind of woman would you like? If you focus on those questions, you'll be able to come up with something to put in an advertisement," Katy assured him. "But don't tell a girl you'll have plenty of time for her when you know you won't. Don't tell her you'll travel with her or relocate if you want to stay home. Be clear. Don't keep things hidden. I did, and I almost lost Garrett because of it."

Alec nodded, taking her words to heart. He knew that he would need to really think about those questions. Not because he didn't know the answers to them, but because he needed to work out how to put them down in a short advertisement. How did you distill the essence of yourself and what you hope for into just a few sentences?

He picked up the large pan of water and potatoes and took it to the stove for Katy. She gave him a thoughtful look, then disappeared from the kitchen for a few moments. When she returned, she had paper, pen, and ink. "Would you like me to help you?" she asked with a kind smile.

CHAPTER 2

September 1879, Boston, Massachusetts

The black gowns fluttered in the breeze, a flurry of caps was thrown into the air, and family and friends laughed and applauded loudly as Harvard's medical students were awarded their diplomas. Anna hadn't been invited to the graduation ceremony, despite finishing in the top three of her class. When it came to the roll call of successful students, read out proudly by the pompous Dean of the school, it was as if she had never existed, but as Anna left the campus of Harvard University, clutching her diploma in her hand—handed to her in the privacy of the administrator's office without any pomp or ceremony—she glanced over without envy at the throng of proud families as they congratulated their sons. They were all doctors now, and Anna didn't need to be part of their old-fashioned rituals. She had a life to lead away from this place.

Though what that might entail, Anna wasn't entirely certain. She had experienced enough dismissal and derision to last her a lifetime. She'd had to work twice as hard as the lowest graduating members of the class to seem even half as good, just because she was a woman and should be content to stay at home and raise fat babies. Anna had proved everyone wrong, her fellow students, the faculty, and the doctors on the wards of Boston's finest hospitals. And it had been worth it. She was now a doctor. It was all she had ever wanted.

Yet, as she walked home, she realized that it wasn't all she'd ever wanted; at least, not entirely. She watched young women pushing baby buggies along the street, cooing to their little ones, and she smiled as couples watched their young children skipping and playing, running rings around their parents. She knew that deep down, in her most secret of hearts, she wanted that, too. A husband who loved her and children she could teach to respect everyone.

Yet it seemed that to have such blessings in her life she would be expected to give up her work, her passion. She loved being a doctor with every fiber of her being. On the wards, she came alive in a way she had never known anywhere else. She loved seeing her patients get well. She enjoyed the challenge of a difficult case, figuring out how she might help. It left a bitter taste in her mouth that the men she had learned and trained with would not be expected to give that up should they have families, but she would.

She let herself into her tiny room. It was all she had been able to afford as she undertook her studies. Her parents were farmers with a tiny acreage a day's ride from the city. They were not wealthy and had struggled to find enough to pay for her classes at the university. She had been responsible for everything else, and it had to be paid for with the earnings she could make from working at the hospital for a pittance they would have been ashamed to offer a male medical student, let alone a fully qualified doctor. But St. Asaph's was the only hospital that had agreed to take her, and she was as glad of the experience she had gained there as she was the funds to pay for her upkeep.

Her landlady had left a copy of the newspaper upon Anna's table. Anna smiled. Mrs. Phelps often left little things for her—a pint of milk, half a loaf of bread she'd baked herself, sometimes some leftover beef stew. It was much appreciated, as every little gift was an expense she could avoid. In return, Anna helped the old woman with any chores that needed a strong arm and tended to her many ailments with kindness and a compassionate ear.

Anna took off her coat and hung it on the hook by the door, yanked off her boots and put them by the fire so they would be warm when she had to go to the hospital later, then set a kettle over the compact stove in the narrow fireplace for some tea. She spooned the loose leaves from the tin above the fireplace into a pot and fetched a cup and saucer from the cupboard in the alcove to the side of the chimney. She sat down at the table and began to read the newspaper while she waited for the kettle to boil.

The world portrayed in the news so often seemed full of doom and gloom to Anna, who tended to look on the bright side of life. But she had always enjoyed the matrimonial pages. She read through the hopeful advertisements of men and women all over the country as they sought love and companionship. Some seemed to want the impossible—a perfect woman or man with every possible asset. Others would be content if someone was able to tolerate them to have some company. Most of the advertisements were placed by men, often in the states to the west; they were cowboys and ranchers who had traveled far afield to make their fortunes but found life lonely without a woman by their side. But Anna had noticed in recent years that more and more women were taking their chance at finding a man who might let them be themselves.

Advertising in such a way had crossed her mind more than once. How would she ever find a man who would accept that she would always be a doctor first and a wife and mother second? She knew from hard-won experience that most men thought her to be unwomanly in her pursuit of a career they believed should be left to men. She had faced much opposition to her wish to become a doctor, from those who simply thought women unsuited to the pressures of such a role, believing them too emotional and too flighty, to those who just thought women belonged in the home, and that was where they should stay.

She had tried to prove both wrong. Anna knew she was good at her work. She had a compassion and concern for her patients that few men showed. Because of that care, she believed she was better at getting to the root cause of a patient's ailment and, therefore, better able to prescribe the correct medicines or surgery required to put it right. Her results had confounded many of her peers—and her superiors—but Anna knew that her success was because she was able to reach her patients in a way her haughty and arrogant colleagues were not.

But, of more importance to her than enjoying the matrimonial ads, Anna needed to find a permanent position. The hospital in Boston could not continue to employ her as a physician's assistant now that she was qualified. Despite her excellent work, the approval of her supervising physician, and her diploma, the board of trustees was unwilling to offer her a permanent position as a physician. She had to find somewhere to go where her being a woman was not an issue for the people with the powers to decide. Anna knew already that there was nowhere in Boston. She would have to look further afield.

She turned to the situations vacant pages and went swiftly to the medical section. She had already sent fifty letters to hospitals and clinics up and down the east coast and had received few replies. And those replies that did arrive had all very politely said that they were not hiring, only for Anna to find out from her fellow students that they had been offered positions. She had always known that it would be hard to achieve her goals, but after years of fighting to get into college, to gain employment in a hospital to support that training, and trying to prove herself every single day, she was tired.

She sighed heavily, just as the kettle came to the boil. She grabbed a cloth from the shelf, lifted the kettle from the stove, and poured the water into the waiting pot. She took the pot to the table, sat back down and resumed her scrutiny of the advertisements while the tea brewed for a few minutes. Several Western towns were advertising for physicians, and Anna decided she did not have the luxury of being choosy. She would apply to every role possible.

She fetched a pen, ink, paper, and her blotter from the box she kept under her wood-framed bed. She poured the tea into the cup and took a sip before beginning to write. By the time the light was dimming, she had written twenty-three letters and had just four more to go. She lit a lamp, then took some bread and ham from the cupboard and ate it while she wrote the last letters. It was almost ten o'clock by the time she had finished. She smiled at the pile of letters ready to mail in the morning, stretched, stood up, and got changed for bed.

Clad in just her nightgown and a robe, she felt a little chilly. She took the lamp and put it on the bedside cabinet, then clambered under the blankets and snuggled up to read the rest of the newspaper. There was a story by Mark Twain, which she read eagerly. She loved to read, though she rarely had time to manage a full novel during her studies, and Mark Twain wrote wonderful stories, full of vivid color and adventure.

But though the tale was fascinating, she kept being drawn back to the matrimonial pages. Why shouldn't she answer a couple of those advertisements or even pay to insert her own? If others could advertise to find exactly what they wished for in a husband or wife, then why shouldn't she? She did not wish to travel through life alone. She longed for a family and a husband who she could love and respect and who would accept and love her in return.

But it was a silly notion, was it not? A young lady such as she would never debase herself in such a way. She was an educated woman. Anna knew she was pretty and had a comely figure, not because she was in any way vain or arrogant, but because the simple truth of her reflection in the mirror confirmed it. She set no store by it. In many ways it had caused her more harm than pleasure, given her goals. Her prettiness had automatically seen her labeled as frivolous and silly by many. Anna had taught her colleagues not to judge anyone upon their appearance alone; or at least, she hoped she had.

She should not need to advertise for a husband. Yet, she was alone because too many men were afraid of a woman of higher intellect and education. No matter how lovely she might be, few men would be willing to marry someone whose career would always come first, as medicine had to. If she stopped practicing for even the shortest while, she would find herself behind on so much; the discipline was ever-changing, with new developments in medicines and procedures happening all the time.

The advertisements were mainly asking for the perfect wife—a homemaker, a loving wife, and a mother—but a few of the advertisers seemed more interested in making a match with someone whose interests were like their own. A few of them even seemed interesting, enjoying reading, learning, music, and theater. It had been years since Anna had the spare time or the money to attend a concert or a play, but she had enjoyed the handful she had been able to attend. She jumped out of bed, grabbed the pile of letters she'd written earlier and her map of America from the box under the bed, then clambered back into bed, shivering a little as she yanked the blankets back up around her body.

Amused at herself, Anna grinned as she unfolded the map and tried to work out where each of the men advertising came from and if any of them matched the positions she had applied for. She noted that five did; at least, they were in the same state. She bit her lip and pondered whether to take a risk and write to them. Anna dithered for a long time, then decided, why not? She had nothing to lose. Anna wrote fluidly and swiftly to them all, then blew out her lamp and settled down to sleep, curling up on her side and wondering what might come of her evening's efforts, trying to imagine a world where she could have it all.

In the morning, she read over the advertisements she had

responded to in the matrimonial column and was about to rip up every letter she'd written because all of it was so futile. She stopped herself when she came to the last advertisement on the page. Anna hadn't written to this gentleman. She didn't even remember reading it, particularly, but she read it very carefully now. The wording was a little blunt, but Anna liked that. This gentleman had not tried to make himself sound better than he was, nor had he overstated his personal and material assets.

She read it aloud to herself, trying to imagine the kind of man that might have written such words.

"A gentleman of Minnesota wishes to write to a young woman with a view to matrimony. Quiet, sometimes solitary, blacksmith passionate about his work, he can offer a comfortable home in a growing town and does not expect a wife to cook and clean but to follow her own will. All responses to be sent to Box 3438, The Boston Times."

She paused and stared at it again. Had he really said he didn't need a wife to undertake wifely duties? Did he truly mean it when he said that he would be content for her to follow her own path? "And does not expect a wife to cook and clean but to follow her own will," she repeated.

"Well, if that is what he wants, then I am that wife. At least, I may be," Anna said as she hurried to the table and quickly scribbled a heartfelt letter to this mysterious man who had said exactly what she longed for a man to say. She could only hope that he truly meant it.

CHAPTER 3

October 1879, Iron Creek, Minnesota

Dear Gentleman of Minnesota,

I find I am at a rather peculiar point in my life, and that has led me in no small way to write to you. You see, I have spent my entire life doing all I could to fulfill my life's ambition: to become a doctor. I say this at the very first because I know that it is probably the most important thing about me.

Medicine is my life. I have had to fight every step of the way to be able to write my name as Dr. Anna Macdonald. As a woman, it is almost impossible to gain entry to college, much less to continue onwards and study law or medicine. I was not afraid of that fight, but it frustrated me that I had to be better than my male peers, to have better grades, and to be better at any clinical tasks to be seen as good enough. Every step of the way, my superiors—except my rather wonderful mentor, Dr.

Skallin; I swear that I would not have made it through without him—tried everything they could to dissuade me, to make me give up on my dream. I did not.

I say this because it is who I am. I am dogged and determined, and I am wholly committed to my profession. No, my vocation. I was born to be a doctor. I find the study and practice of it fascinating, frightening, stimulating, and vibrant in its complexity. I cannot imagine ever doing anything else.

Yet, I long for a family, too. To have a husband to love and care for, to respect and admire—and who will do the same in return. I am passionate and forthright, to my detriment, perhaps. In a world where women are supposed to be gentle and acquiescent, I rather stand out!

I do not long for a home to run or to pick up my husband's dirty socks; rather, I wish to continue my work as my husband continues his. Why should a woman have to leave a job that gives her satisfaction and pleasure upon marriage while a man does not? The unfairness of such an arrangement never fails to grate upon me, I'm afraid.

It may be some time before my work pays sufficiently for me to hire a housekeeper and a nanny to take care of the children, given I shall have to build a practice from scratch, no doubt, but I will be glad to strive toward that if I am blessed to find a man who understands this and supports it.

I know that many men might be put off by my direct manner, and I apologize for it if it has caused any offense. I understand that and know I could do more to temper it—at *least upon first acquaintance! I also know how few men truly want an educated wife, so I will understand if I never hear anything from you, though I do sincerely hope I will.*

Yours most faithfully,

Dr. Anna Macdonald

Alec shook his head as he read the letter. This young woman was indeed direct. He had not expected anyone quite like her when he'd placed the advertisement, but he had hoped. She was so honest, so frank, and she had a vocation she was passionate about, as he did. She would not mind him being gone at all hours, slaving over the fire of the forge, as she would be working all hours herself, should she find a suitable opportunity nearby. And though she had not said that she wanted to have a mother-in-law running her home and raising her children, she had seemed very open to the idea of someone being present to do that work. There was much to still learn about each other and much to consider, but for a first letter, this was at least reassuring, though he doubted that many men would have read it as such.

He quickly penned a response and hurried along the street to mail it. He paid the postage to Hank Wilson, who seemed eager to know who he was writing to. Alec remained his reticent self and said little, without being rude, and departed without having given the talkative postmaster anything to add to his store of local gossip. Feeling hopeful that there might be someone out there for him after all, he went about the rest of his day with a spring in his step.

When he returned home, it was late. The house was cold and dark. His mother was still in Chicago as his aunt's health had taken a turn for the worst. Alec did not mind. He was glad she had not been around when the first reply to his advertisement arrived. Mama was bound to overreact and accuse him of doing something behind her back or trying to supplant her; or worse, she would become so invested in the idea of him taking a bride that he would not be permitted to make the choice for himself should anyone other than Dr. Macdonald write to him.

After lighting the lamps, Alec lit a fire in the grate of the large kitchen fireplace and then lit the stove, too. By the time he'd had a wash and put on some clean clothes, the room was warm. He made himself a simple meal of steak and potatoes. He put the food onto a plate and sank into his armchair by the fire to eat it. Though he usually ate at the table, he needed a little comfort after a long day in the forge. He ate the food down quickly, then re-read Dr. Macdonald's letter. She was certainly feisty. She knew her mind, and she was not afraid to fight for what she wanted. To have achieved all she had, she must have had to fight hard and long. He admired her for that immensely. He tucked her letter away in his pocket and quickly washed the dishes before retiring to bed.

He slept soundly and woke with the dawn, as he always did. He washed his face, dressed, and went downstairs. After pulling on his jacket, he headed to the forge. Once there, he stoked the furnace and added plenty of fuel to keep it burning all day. As it heated up, he returned home and fixed himself some eggs and bacon, strong coffee, and some bread with Mama's homemade blackberry preserves.

Mrs. Jellicoe was waiting for him when he returned to the forge. Alec had made some gates for her and her husband a while ago, and they had been delighted with them. She beamed at him as he walked into the yard, and he smiled back at her. Mrs. Jellicoe was sweet and pretty and had rambunctious twin boys who took up all her time. "What a pleasure," he exclaimed.

She blushed sweetly. "It is kind of you to say so," she said. "I am afraid that the twins have made rather a nuisance of themselves again."

"They are young and determined to explore their world," Alec said politely. The boys were known all around town for their wild ways. Though only barely walking, they still managed to get themselves into all manner of trouble. "Better that than a pair of dullards."

"I suppose so, but it is getting rather expensive," Mrs. Jellicoe said with a rueful look.

"How can I help?" Alec asked her gently.

"They have somehow swung your beautiful gates right off their hinges," she said, shaking her head in disbelief. "I do hope it will be possible to fix them."

"I am sure it will be, and I will do all I can to make them twin-proof," he assured her. "I can come now if that suits you?"

She nodded, and the two of them wandered slowly along

Main Street to the Jellicoe's fine townhouse. It was one of the largest in town. Mr. Jellicoe owned a newspaper that ran editions in all the local towns and cities. He'd grown it from nothing and was now reaping the benefits of his years of hard work.

After they arrived at the house, Alec surveyed the damage. Mrs. Jellicoe was right; the wrought-iron gates were hanging from their hinges in a way Alec could hardly believe. The twins had done the work that four strong horses might struggle to achieve.

"It might take me a week or two. I have a lot of other work as people ensure their carriages and gigs are as safe as can be for the winter, but I'll bring the cart and fetch them later today," Alec said, walking around the gates and marveling at the twins' destructive powers. He prayed that if he ever had children of his own that they wouldn't be quite as wild as the Jellicoe twins.

"Thank you," Mrs. Jellicoe said, clearly delighted. "I cannot tell you how grateful I am."

"It's my job, Mrs. Jellicoe," Alec said. "I must confess that I thought these gates would be strong enough to hold back a herd of buffalo."

"My twins make buffalo look sweet and cuddly," Mrs. Jellicoe joked. "I love them, but they are devils. If only Katy hadn't decided to leave us. She was so good with them. They rarely dared give her any trouble."

"She can be a little stern for all her kindness," Alec said, thinking of how strong and capable his friend's new wife could be.

"Yes, and I am just too soft. And they know it," Mrs. Jellicoe lamented.

Alec returned to his forge and started work. He repaired wheels and made new ones all day until he was bored, then he shod horses and repaired tools for the townsfolk before he headed home late again. Unexpectedly, the house was full of light when he arrived. He went inside to the warmth and the smell of his mother's cooking. He sighed. His time of peace and tranquility was over. Mama had returned.

She appeared in the doorway of the kitchen when she heard him enter, beaming her delight at seeing him. He embraced her warmly. "Welcome home," he said. "How is Aunt Lilah?"

"She is doing much better now, praise the Lord, and I am glad to be back," she replied, her head upon his chest, her arms tight around his waist. "I missed you terribly."

Alec smiled and extricated himself from the hug. "I should go and wash up," he said, knowing her rules for how to present himself for dinner all too well.

"Hurry along; the pie will spoil otherwise," Mama said with an indulgent smile. It was as if he were still a boy and had been out playing in the mud.

With a heavy sigh, Alec mounted the stairs. He wished that she might have at least sent some warning of her arrival. No doubt she had been appalled by the lack of cleaning he'd done while she'd been gone, and she undoubtedly knew that he'd turned down many of the kind offers of meals that she had lined up for him with their neighbors. He would, of course, get a scolding. Yet despite it all, he truly had missed her. She made his life easier, at least in the most practical of ways, even if there were times when he wished that she would go home to her own house in Grand Marais.

She was in a sparkling mood over supper and was good enough to withhold all the things she wasn't happy about that had happened while she was gone. She seemed lighter somehow than when she'd left, as if having someone to look after who really needed her had given her a new lease on life. Perhaps she was as bored keeping his house as he was stifled by her always being there. He was not a difficult man to care for; he was barely present, so he didn't need her. Not really. And she knew that.

"Mama, do you ever wish to perhaps do something more than just keep house for me?" he asked, blurting it out at a time when she could hardly have been expecting it. She was in the middle of telling him all about Aunt Lilah's bedsores.

"I don't know what you mean," she said, genuinely baffled. "I love taking care of you."

"I know you do, but there isn't much for you to do, is there? I mean, not really."

She pursed her lips and furrowed her brow for a moment. "I suppose not. But I don't know what else you think I might do. It's not as if a woman like me could take a position somewhere else and still keep house for you here."

"But what if you could?" he asked curiously, a thought beginning to form in his mind.

"I suppose it would be nice to be a little busier. But I am not qualified to do much else. I've only ever been a wife and mother."

"Oh, that will be all the skill you need," Alec said with a grin, thinking he might just pay Mrs. Jellicoe another visit in the morning. If the twins could withstand the insistence upon discipline and order that his mother demanded, they were braver men than he—and they were just children.

CHAPTER 4

November 1879, Boston, Massachusetts

The weather was inclement, with stormy skies and more rain than Anna could remember. She normally enjoyed the fall, with its russets and golds and often cool but sunny days, but not this year. This year she was anxious for her future, and the weather seemed to be reflecting her mood. She had received only a handful of replies to her inquiries. Most of those that she had received regarding positions as a physician had been polite rejections, and the letters she'd written to find herself a husband had either been ignored, or the men who had written back seemed dull and entirely too pompous. Every one of them was supportive of her achievements, at least right up to the point where they expected her to give up her work, should she find any, once she was a wife and mother.

Dr. Skallin, the man from whom she'd learned almost everything and who had fought so hard to get her a position in the hospital, had somehow managed to get her a temporary position undertaking administrative tasks for his ward. It wasn't ideal, but it meant he could sneak her into procedures from time to time and stop by to go through difficult cases with her as they had done throughout her training. It kept her mind sharp and her skills at least vaguely current. And it paid enough to keep the roof over her head and food in her belly.

She would never forget his kindness and support. From the very first time they'd met, over six years ago, he had been happy to educate her and had allowed her to work with him. She was so grateful for his agreeing to mentor her and supervise her training, as well as his assistance in convincing his colleagues to take her onto their wards so she might experience as much as possible during her training. But it was the friendship he had offered so freely when others so often shunned her that meant the most to her. Anna would miss him terribly when she had to leave. She knew that there would be no hope of her finding a place in Boston, so leave she must.

As the days and weeks had passed with no possibility of a position anywhere, Anna had begun to fear that despite all her efforts to the contrary, she might never truly fulfill her dreams. Being a woman precluded her from being a suitable physician. Being a physician precluded her from being a suitable wife. It felt like there was no way around it. Everywhere she looked, there was a large wall in front of her stopping her from moving forward. She hated it.

A knock on her door made Anna jump. The handle rattled, and the hinges squeaked as it was pushed open. Anna turned to see Mrs. Phelps' face peering around the door. "Good morning, my dear," she said. "You have visitors. I left them in my parlor with some tea."

"Visitors?" Anna said, surprised. She wasn't expecting anyone.

"Yes, come on down when you're ready."

Giving no more information than that, the diminutive old woman disappeared, leaving Anna wondering who might wish to call on her. She had few friends here in the city, after all. Her fellow students had excluded her from their society, the few people she knew at the hospital would not dream of calling on her unannounced, and she'd had little time to make so much as an acquaintance anywhere else. Perhaps it was Albert, though she thought he was wrapped up in a very important court hearing that was scheduled to last for some weeks. He never had time for anything else when he was in court.

She brushed her hair quickly and reached for a shawl, then made her way downstairs. Just over halfway down the stairs, she peered into the open door right ahead of her. She chuckled and bit her lip, full of pure delight, when she saw who was waiting for her in Mrs. Phelps' parlor. Her parents had made the trip from their farm. It was a little over twenty miles from the city, and Anna could count on one hand the number of times they had left it during her lifetime. Certainly, any occasion when they had left it together was rare, as they always needed to leave someone behind to keep an eye on things.

"Whatever are you doing here?" she asked, taking the last steps at a run and rushing into the warm front room. She flung herself into their arms and hugged them both tightly. They both looked overjoyed to see her, and she drank in their love and affection as though parched.

"We finished the harvest in record time, so we had a few days to spare. What better way to make use of them than to come and see our clever girl?" her father said proudly as he embraced her. He then held her away from him so he could look her over. "You've lost weight. Do you not have enough food here?"

"You know what I am like when I am studying, I forget the time of day entirely," Anna explained. "During my final exams, I don't think I ate a bite between my nerves and the need to cram every last bit of knowledge into my head." She laughed, not wanting them to worry, but she had also struggled to find the money to pay for food as there had been no shifts at the hospital during those final months of her time in medical school.

"I know you graduated a while ago now, but we couldn't leave then," her mother explained. "You know how busy things are over the summer and into the early days of fall. But we are so proud of you."

"Mom, I do know," Anna said. She kissed her mother's ruddy cheek. "And it does not matter that you couldn't come earlier. I am just so happy to see you both now."

"We thought we could take you out for a special lunch to celebrate your becoming a doctor," her father said, his eyes twinkling at her the way they always did. He had always been her biggest and most enthusiastic supporter. He'd encouraged her to reach for the stars and never let other people's expectations get in the way of her dreams. Her mom had always been a little more circumspect. She knew just how hard it was to be a woman in a man's world, and she had feared for Anna. And rightly so, as it turned out. All her mother's concerns about Anna never being accepted fully anywhere seemed to be all too real now.

"That would be wonderful," Anna said. Receiving her diploma had fallen more than a little flat at the time. Her classmates had celebrated without her, and there had been nobody there to make an occasion out of it for her.

"I thought we might go to the Crawford Rooms," her father said with a wink. "One of the gentlemen I sold grain to arranged it all for us. He's a regular patron there." Anna smiled. Mom had always wanted to go to the fashionable dining rooms after seeing an article in the newspaper about the number of well-to-do people who attended them. "Mr. Anderson was delighted with the quality of the grain and was glad to do me a favor."

Anna was proud that her father was so well respected and

so excited about his trip to the big city. Boston was a place he usually dreaded having to visit. "That is most kind of him. It would be lovely. But it's frightfully expensive."

"I am well aware of that," he said, puffing out his chest proudly. "We've been saving a little, and the harvest has been good. And frankly, I think you deserve the very best after all your years of hard work."

Anna was touched, and she felt tears pricking at her eyes. "Well, I'd best go and change my dress," she said, her voice a little choked with emotion. "I can't go to the elegant Crawford Rooms without being properly dressed for the occasion."

She left them in Mrs. Phelps' parlor and went back up to her room to change into her Sunday best. It was a rich blue velvet gown her parents had given her when she left for college so she would have something fine to wear to any events at Harvard. She had never worn it, but she would never tell them that there had been no call for it before now. It looked as good as new, though, so she would have to come up with a good reason for that.

When she returned downstairs, Mrs. Phelps was standing in the hallway, holding a small handful of letters. The mail had obviously just been delivered, and the kindly old lady was rifling through it to see who it was for. She always delivered everything to each room herself rather than leaving it on the hall table for her tenants to collect on their way in or out of the house. She insisted nobody's post ever got lost that way, and she was probably right.

"There's six for you today, Anna," she said, her eyebrows raised as she handed them to Anna. The older woman's reaction to a flurry of mail arriving for Anna wasn't entirely surprising. Anna had barely received more than a few letters a year since she'd arrived, but that had changed recently. "D'you want them now, or would you rather I put them up in your room for later?"

Anna desperately wanted to open them there and then, but she did not want to ruin the special pleasure of her parents' visit if the letters were more rejections. Of course, if one of them held good news, there would be another thing for them to celebrate, but Anna knew all too well that such an outcome was unlikely. "Can you take them upstairs for me? I don't want anything to ruin my mood."

"Of course, my dear. Now, you go and have a wonderful afternoon with your family. I look forward to hearing all about it. The Crawford Rooms, eh? How lovely."

Anna peered into Mrs. Phelps' parlor. "Shall we go?" Her parents joined her in the hallway and took their coats and hats from the stand where Mrs. Phelps had hung them carefully, and the three of them made their way out onto the street, where her father waved down a passing hackney cab to take them to the restaurant.

The Crawford Rooms were on the corner of Court and Brattle Streets and housed in a beautiful, five-story building, with elegantly decorated windows, with those on each floor a slightly different shape. And the building had an elevator.

Anna knew that her fellow students had often arranged private parties in the salons there, and many regularly dined there with their wealthy and influential parents.

Anna tried hard not to gaze around her like a country girl as they entered the opulent surroundings and were shown to their table by the maître d,' though her mother and father struggled to appear so composed. Her mom was particularly enamored with the huge crystal chandeliers and the way the light from them was reflected by the vast, gold-framed mirrors everywhere. Her dad was more interested in the marble floors and the fluted columns in the hallway, as well as the grand staircase that wound its way up through the building.

The drapes in each of the adjoining rooms were thick velvet or luxurious damask, the tablecloths a heavy white cotton that was so soft Anna could hardly believe it was possible. The silverware gleamed and fresh flowers were set in colorful but tasteful displays upon every table. A liveried waiter appeared behind the maître d' with a cotton cloth over his arm and a silver tray with three glasses filled with a pale red liquid upon it in his hand. He bowed to them as he placed the glasses before each of their seats, then pulled out Anna's chair as the maître d' pulled out her mother's. Her father pulled out his own chair, and they all sat down, the attending staff adjusting the seats precisely so that Anna and her mother were at the perfect distance from the table to eat comfortably.

"Mr. Anderson requested that you try this apéritif upon your arrival," the maître d' said politely, his tone soft and calm. He had the trace of an accent, making Anna wonder where he came from. "He ordered it especially for you and wishes to tell you that your meal today will be put on his account."

Her father shook his head in disbelief. "Well, that is mighty kind of him, though it is too much of a gift for us to accept."

The maître d' smiled. "He said you would say precisely that, sir, and so I am to give you this." He handed Anna's father a letter. "I shall return with the details of today's menu and a list of suitable wines to match in a few moments. Enjoy your luncheon with us today." With that, he and the waiter left the table.

Anna watched her father open the letter and begin to read what was inside. "Well, I never!" he exclaimed. "Oh, my!"

"What is it?" Anna asked him, impatient to find out what was making her father so incredulous—and so happy.

"Mr. Anderson got a better price for my grain than he had expected and has made a fine profit. He wants me to have my share and so has left instructions to make payment to me at his lawyers' offices. The amount will be enough to buy that plot of land next to ours that we've had our eye on." He shook his head in disbelief. "I knew he was a decent and honorable man, but this is much more than I could ever have expected."

"It is certainly rare that any man would do such a thing," Anna agreed.

"Most would just take the additional profits themselves," her mother said, nodding her agreement with Anna.

"So, we have even more to celebrate than we thought," her father said, raising his glass so they might make a toast. "To all our futures. May they be bright, healthy, and happy."

"To our futures," Anna and her mother echoed and took a sip of the slightly fizzing beverage. It had a hint of strawberry to it, but Anna was certain that the base of the drink was champagne. The bubbles tickled her nose, but she decided that she liked it much more than she should. It was a taste she could certainly get used to, though it would be better for her if she did not. Whatever lay in her future, the money to buy champagne was not likely to be a part of it.

CHAPTER 5

November 1879, Boston Massachusetts

Mrs. Phelps had been kind enough to make up her spare room while the family was out at lunch, so Mr. and Mrs. Macdonald could stay for the night. Feeling completely full after their magnificent feast and a slow walk back through the city to the boarding house, Anna's parents agreed that they were tired and wished to retire. Anna kissed them and hugged them tightly, then watched them make their way to their room for the night. She glanced at the clock behind her and smiled. It was barely six o'clock. Anna's parents were early-to-bed, early-to-rise folk. Their journey to the city must have started at the very crack of dawn, and they would be leaving early the next day, so an earlier night than usual was not entirely surprising.

Anna retired to her room, too, where she opened the letters Mrs. Phelps had left on her table. The first two were rejections for the positions she had applied for in Florida and California. She was saddened and frustrated in equal measure but not surprised. She set them aside and sighed heavily. She was beginning to doubt if she would ever find a place where she could practice medicine. The world seemed set against the idea of a lady doctor.

The third was from a cattle rancher in Utah. He seemed to need a slave rather than a wife. Anna immediately dismissed him as a future husband. His views were even more archaic than most. But the fourth and fifth letters were particularly interesting as they both came from South Dakota. One was from a hotel owner whose advertisement for a wife she had responded to, and the other was from the mayor of a newly incorporated town who would be more than happy to consider her for the position of town physician.

She read both letters again, starting with the position at Copperton Mill. The letter outlined that she would need to begin a new practice there. The town currently had no doctor but had grown too big for those in nearby towns to keep serving its populace. The town council had big plans for their little mining town, including the arrival of the railway there in the next year. It was a definite prospect and one that was rather exciting to Anna. It also gave her a huge sense of relief to finally find that she was wanted somewhere. She felt her tense muscles begin to relax just a little, and a slight smile curved her lips as she considered the opportunity in front of her.

She couldn't keep that smile from her face as she re-read the letter from the hotel owner, though not because of what was in this letter. The gentleman's name was Derek Thompson, and he not only owned the hotel in Great Falls but also had a saloon and boarding house in Deadwood, as well as a fine hotel in Claytonville, where he lived. Such things were indeed admirable, and he was right to boast of them, but they did little to impress Anna. She was more interested in what else he had to say. From what he'd written, he liked being busy, and with having so many enterprises to run, Anna didn't doubt he managed it all quite well. He admitted he was not the stay-at-home type, that a wife would need to be able to amuse herself in his absence but promised that he would make it up to her upon his return. He didn't have many interests outside his work, but that didn't bother Anna too greatly. He admitted to enjoying a show when he was in the city and said it would be nice if she might accompany him on some of his travels from time to time.

It wasn't exactly the most romantic of letters, but Anna rather liked that. He seemed honest and straightforward, with an eye to his future. He enjoyed his work, and it occupied a lot of his time. She would not be expected to have to cater to his every need as he was so rarely in one place. But a man with such a busy schedule would have little space in his life for much else, and that could well mean that she would end up bringing up any children they might have completely alone. On the other hand, his wealth should mean that hiring help would not be a problem. He didn't mention anything about her being a doctor, but Anna did not see any reason to be concerned about that at this point. He had focused his letter upon the questions she had asked of him, so it was all about himself.

As she got ready for bed, Anna wondered how far it was from Claytonville to Copperton Mill. If it wasn't too far, a pairing might be worth considering. However, she wasn't sure if she would wish for either of them. Copperton Mill was a very exciting prospect, but there were concerns. As a small town with no other physician, they really needed someone with experience. Anna had barely finished her education and training, so she wasn't entirely sure if she was ready to work alone without anyone with greater experience and knowledge to guide her. And as for Mr. Thompson, a man who would almost never be present wasn't entirely ideal. But combined, they could be a good compromise. Anna wrote back to them both immediately.

She opened the final letter once she'd settled herself into bed. It was from a gentleman in a place called Iron Creek in Minnesota.

Dear Dr. Macdonald,

Thank you for your very candid letter. I hope you won't mind if I begin this letter by congratulating you upon your becoming a doctor. I can only imagine how hard it must have been to even gain a place at Harvard, much less the many years of study you have since had to go through.

My parents wished for me to follow in my father's footsteps and become a doctor, or perhaps a lawyer if I truly could not bear the thought of medicine. There is not a man in the family on my father's side who is not one or the other. However, it was never something that appealed to me, though I respect those who are prepared to work and study so hard for so long to undertake such arduous roles. Had I chosen to follow such a path, I fear it may well have been much simpler for me than it must have been for you.

I fought back against my family's plans for me, though, and now I live in a small town in Minnesota, not far from the Sawtooth Mountains. People call them mountains, but they are not majestic like what people speak of the Rockies, or the Alps in Europe. They lack the craggy sharpness of such ranges. Instead, they have a more rolling majesty, and because the plains in this part of the country are so vast and so flat, they seem small when seen along the horizon as you approach them from the forests and flatlands to the west of us.

Iron Creek began life as a trading post and has grown steadily over the past few years. The area here is rich in iron deposits, and the mines about an hour's ride from here supply the mills and foundries in Duluth. There are many lakes within a day's ride or less, and Lake Superior is right here, no more than an hour's ride. The land is beautiful, in its own way. It doesn't have much, not even in Grand Marais—the nearest big town—but what we have serves us well.

Defying my parents' intentions, I trained as a blacksmith. And I love my work with a passion I could never have mustered for a more academic profession. I work with both iron and steel. I must, as I am the only smith within forty miles. I have had to learn many more techniques since I completed my apprenticeship because of this, and I am happy to do so. I enjoy the challenge of learning new things.

Like yours, the hours I work are long. The forge is a stern mistress and requires constant tending to ensure she remains at the perfect temperature to temper the metal so that I can shape it. Because of this, it is hard for me to leave it for any extended period, so I am not the man for you if you long for a life of constant companionship.

However, if you could be content with a man who enjoys reading, spending time with his family and friends, and who works too hard, please write back to me. I know that I would be glad to meet a woman with a life of her own, so I need not fret about her being bored and or needing a man by her side at all times. To be blessed with the knowledge that a wife is following her own path in her own way would give me great happiness.

Yours most sincerely

Alec Jenks

His words were simple yet vivid and full of meaning, and

they gave Anna a real sense of the man. Alec Jenks was a man of passion, not reason. He was happy in his profession, something few men of her acquaintance ever seemed to be, and he was happy for her to follow her vocation. She instantly liked him. But she did not know if there would be a possibility for work in the little town he spoke of so fondly, or even in a nearby town. It seemed a little too rude to ask such a thing outright; it would make it seem as if her interest in him would only be ignited should there be an opportunity for her career as well.

She picked up her pen and dipped it into the inkwell, pausing for a moment as she thought about how to reply. Anna certainly did not wish to seem too forward, too bold, or in any way rude. She wanted this gentleman to like her back, but that somehow seemed an impossible task to achieve with only the written word to help her cause. She started to write, then stopped and scribbled up the words she put down many, many times before she finally composed something she was pleased with.

Dear Mr. Jenks,

Thank you for your wonderful letter. Your home sounds fabulous. I would so like to hear more about it. Are there many animals and birds nearby? I am a farmer's daughter and, though I love my work, I miss being on the land, watching all of nature unfold before me. The changing of the seasons and all that it brings fascinates me almost as much as the changes within the human body that bring about disease and imbal-

ance. *Of course, the seasons pass in the city, but it is not the same.*

I am so glad that you are not concerned about my wish to continue my work. I should hate to have to give it up. Though, should we decide that we are a suitable pairing, I am unsure as to whether I would be able to find work near to your home. I have not seen any advertisements in the press requesting doctors in Minnesota, but I will continue to search for something in the hope that we might someday meet in person.

I have little to talk about, other than my studies. They have taken up such a large part of my life for so long I have had little time for anything else, so I am rather at a loss as to what I might tell you about myself. Like you, my work is my life.

Though, I suppose I can just tell you about my day today. My parents arrived in Boston early this afternoon, completely unexpectedly, to celebrate my graduation with me. I cannot tell you how delighted I was to see them. I have not seen them since Christmas, though they only live a day's ride from here. Their farm is small but had a fine harvest this year, and the merchant they sold the grain to managed to sell it for a higher price than expected. To our stunned surprise, he insisted that my father take a share of those profits. He also arranged for us to dine in a fancy restaurant for lunch and insisted on paying the bill. The food was heavenly, like nothing I have ever tasted before, and we were waited upon as if we were royalty. It was quite the occasion. I don't think I have ever seen my parents so happy. And they are so proud of me.

I find myself unable to tell them how concerned I am that all their sacrifices may yet come to nothing if I cannot find a position somewhere. It seems that few towns and hospitals wish to employ a lady doctor. All my classmates had no difficulties finding a position, even those who barely managed to pass any of their classes. It infuriates me to know that I am the better doctor but, because they are men, they have the work that should be mine.

I do not know why I am telling you this, given you are a stranger to me at this juncture. Perhaps it is because writing seems somehow more intimate, and so I can say so much more than I ever would in person. But my troubles are not yet yours, so I do not expect you to have an answer to my quandary. I do hope that my frankness does not stop you from writing to me again. I rather enjoyed receiving your letter.

Yours most hopefully,
Dr. Anna Macdonald

ANNA WASN'T sure why it seemed so easy to tell this man the things she had kept to herself for so long, but from the moment she had read his advertisement, she had known that there was something trustworthy about him—on paper at least. With his letter, that feeling had only grown. He seemed to understand how hard things had been for her and respected her for pushing onwards despite all those travails. He was not afraid of her or cowed by her in any way. He appeared to respect her as a person in her own right. Anna liked that.

Despite the few other replies she sent out, Anna prayed Alec Jenks would write back to her. She liked him far more than the rather dull hotel owner in South Dakota. But she was a practical woman. There was a position for her in the Dakotas. Mr. Thompson may well be considerably more affable in person, so there was no reason to dismiss either man at this stage. She would see what might come from more extensive correspondence and would perhaps arrange a trip to meet with representatives of Copperton Mill to discuss the work expected of her in person. Maybe she could convince all the relevant parties to meet her in Chicago, where their trains and other transport would most likely diverge.

But that was a plan for the future. She did not have the funds to go anywhere immediately, and despite her parents' recent good fortune, she would never ask them for a penny that might take her even further from them. She knew how much it hurt them to only see her the handful of times during the year when she had enough time to go home. If she lived in South Dakota or Minnesota, such visits would be all but impossible. She knew they would not take the news well, though they would understand, as they always did, that she had to follow the path she had fought so hard for.

No, she would have to try to convince the hospital to give her more work so she could save enough to travel across the country and find out what fate had in store for her. She was still unsure whether any of this was a good idea, but at that precise moment in time, she did not have any other ideas. She did not mind the idea of going somewhere new where she could build a new life, hopefully without the prejudice she had experienced in Boston, but she was also sad that it would mean saying goodbye to her family, who she loved dearly and who had already given up so much so her dreams could come true.

CHAPTER 6

Christmas 1879, Iron Creek, Minnesota

It was almost Christmas when Alec realized how much time had passed without a response from Dr. Macdonald. He knew that having such a strong response to such a short letter was possibly irrational, yet he was saddened that she had not wished to correspond with him any further after his last letter. He had rather enjoyed her feisty and honest letter and had hoped to get to know her better. Perhaps she had decided that he was not for her after she had received his letter in return. Perhaps she had been made an offer she could not refuse, either by another man or more likely from someone offering her a position somewhere. Either way, he couldn't help feeling that he had missed out on something that could have been very special.

As he pounded the iron over the anvil, he pondered

whether he wished to try again. He had received several other responses around the time that he'd received Dr. Macdonald's, but none of them had intrigued him in the way hers had. And there had been no replies lately. At least he couldn't remember any more arriving since his mother had returned from Chicago. He supposed that such things would peter out in this way, as new advertisements were posted and new editions of the newspapers printed. It was frustrating that he was no closer to finding someone to love now than he had been all those months ago.

He had too much work to dwell upon it, though, so he continued through the long list of tasks the townsfolk had requested he finish for them as soon as possible. He arrived home, with aching arms and a sore back, at ten o'clock. In his absence, his mother had filled the house with garlands of evergreens and holly rich with winterberries, ready for Christmas. It made the house smell as fresh as the forest and look completely festive. It lifted his mood almost immediately. He took off his coat and gloves, then pulled off his boots with an energetic tug before approaching her at the stove and kissing her cheek. "How do you always do this?" he asked.

"Do what?" she asked, feigning ignorance, then giggled.

"All of this? Every year, Christmas appears as if by magic."

"Ah, I just don't tell you when I intend to do it. Besides, you are usually so busy that you barely know what day it is, so when I set the decorations around the house on Christmas Eve, as I do every year, you are always surprised." She grinned at him and reached up to pinch his cheek affectionately. "Now, go and wash up. I've left a jug of hot water on the washstand for you. Supper will be ready when you return, and we can attend Mass at midnight. Father Paul has come from Grand Marais for us this year."

She made it sound as though the catholic priest came to Iron Creek especially for them, but many other Catholics were living in the town, too. Alec did as he'd been told. He washed and put on his best suit and shirt. He would tie a cloth around his neck to be sure he didn't spill anything down it at supper, which turned out to be a steak pie that was filling and delicious after his long day at the forge. Alec ate two large helpings before declaring he was full.

"I'm glad," his mother said, looking at him proudly. "I know I have said it many times, but thank you, again, for speaking with Mrs. Jellicoe to see if she would appreciate a little help. The twins are terrors, but they are so full of life. I enjoy it very much." Her eyes sparkled with happiness. Alec was glad she seemed to have finally found something to give her joy again. It had been too long. She smiled more often now and had a spring in her step. She'd also regained her appetite and ate as heartily as she used to and was no longer skin and bones. She winked at him. "Perhaps one day, I will have some plump little grandchildren of my own to care for."

Her tone was loaded with emphasis, and Alec could feel the weight of her expectations fall upon his shoulders. Perhaps he would have to place a second advertisement after all. He had disappointed his mother in so many ways, and he did not dare let her down by never giving her grandchildren. But it was not a night to dwell on those things he had not provided. If it was indeed the night before Christmas, he needed to find a gift for his mother.

"I will be back shortly," he announced to his mother. "I need to check on something at the forge." She smiled indulgently as if to say that she knew that he had forgotten how close it was to Christmas, and she didn't mind that he hadn't remembered to get her a gift. "I shall be back in time to take you to mass."

He disappeared into the night, wondering what he could possibly give her. She was not an easy woman to choose gifts for. She always swore that she had everything she wanted and needed, so Alec was often stumped as to how he might please her. When he was younger, and during the years of his apprenticeship, he had made her things. But such an option was not so easy now as she had every item that could be made from iron or steel a woman could possibly need.

Her birthday was in the summer. That at least gave him the option of gathering armfuls of wildflowers and decorating the house with them, but such things weren't available to him in winter. As he wandered onto Main Street, racking his brains, he spotted Judd Barclay, the owner of the general store. He had obviously just closed the store for the holiday, the blinds were down, and he was locking the door as Alec approached him. "You look troubled," Judd said. He smiled at Alec and held out his hand.

Alec took it and shook it warmly. "I forgot a gift for Mama. Again," he said. Judd had been his salvation on more occasions than Alec could count.

"No, you did not," Judd said, his eyes sparkling with mischief. "Don't you recall, you asked me to hold back that fine new mixing bowl and the pretty scarf your mother admired a few weeks ago?" Alec knew he'd done no such thing, but his friend had clearly taken note of the things his mother had admired while she'd been in his store.

Alec shook his head in disbelief. Judd was a good friend indeed. "I do not know what I would do without you," he said, clapping Judd on the back. Judd winced a little. Alec gave him a rueful look; in his excitement, he often forgot his strength.

"I've even gift wrapped them for you," Judd added. "I left them in my wood store, around back. I was just coming to slip a note through your door."

"I will gladly pay you double, my friend," Alec said, utterly relieved and truly grateful.

"No need, but you could take a look at my barn door when you have time? The old hinges have rusted away to almost nothing. Some new ones would be nice."

"They are yours, along with a new door handle and anything else you might need."

After a quick detour to Judd's wood store around back, Alec took the neatly wrapped parcel back home and hid it in his own barn. He went back inside, where he found his mother sitting in a rocker by the stove in the kitchen, dressed in a floral dress with a white lace collar, waiting for him to arrive. She stood up when the door opened and picked up her gloves and hat from the table. "We will be late if we don't hurry," she said, glancing up at the clock.

Alec looked, too. It was almost half-past eleven. Even if they walked as slowly as a snail, they'd be there with plenty of time to spare, but he knew his mother liked to talk with their neighbors a little before mass began, so, without argument, he offered her his arm, and the two of them made their way to the back room of the saloon.

It was an incongruous place for a mass to be held, but there was no Roman Catholic chapel in Iron Creek, and the Presbyterian church was not deemed to be suitable for some reason that made no sense to Alec. He attended mass because it pleased his mother. Alec believed in God quite resolutely, but his faith was not tied to one particular church. He could as happily worship on the banks of Lake Superior or in the Sawtooth Mountains as in a church.

His mother greeted everyone cheerfully, asking after their families, then came and whispered the most salacious gossip about some of them. It never failed to shock him that his mother could at times be so two-faced. That she would be that way at a church service was even more strange to him. He believed that his faith made him more considerate of others and kinder and gentler toward those that he might not agree with or who didn't share his ways, but it seemed it made his mother rather judgmental.

Father Paul delivered the mass with his beautiful soft, lilting Irish accent. At times, raucous cries and the sound of the tinny old piano could be heard as the less religious celebrations next door in the saloon grew more fevered. Father Paul did not so much as flinch; he just continued to recite the words that everyone present knew by heart, then they all received the final blessing and began to disperse.

"Shall I make some hot chocolate, Mama?" he asked her as they let themselves into the house and took off their hats and coats. His mother smiled and patted his cheek.

"I'd like that, and perhaps a slice of fruit cake. There's some in the larder."

"Mmmm," Alec said. He happily set about pouring milk into a pan and looking for the chocolate and cake in the large, walk-in cupboard at the cooler end of the kitchen. He made the chocolate the way his mother liked it best, rich and sweet, and set it down, steaming hot, in front of her at the kitchen table. She had sliced the fruit cake; a thick hunk was plated before his seat, and a smaller slice for her.

They ate and drank their Christmas Eve treats as they had always done, ever since Alec was a little boy. It always felt special, but it was also a little sad now that his father no longer sat in his place at the head of the table. Alec knew they both missed his father more at Christmas and on birthdays, so he waited up with his mother for some time even though no words passed between them. Eventually, though, his yawns grew too intense to ignore. "Good night," he said to his mother when the clock chimed two. He kissed the top of her head and placed his big hand on her tiny shoulder as he passed by her chair. "Merry Christmas."

"Good night," she said, reaching up and clasping his hand where it lay. She gave it a squeeze and let go. "I think I'll stay up for a while. I'd like to enjoy a little peace and quiet." Alec knew she was thinking of his father. This time, after church, was one they had always shared. A moment of peace and contemplation. It had been a special time for them, and Alec knew that no matter how many years passed, it would always be a difficult time for his mother.

CHAPTER 7

January 1880, Boston, Massachusetts

Christmas had been a joy. Anna had gone home to the farm, and her parents had spoiled her with love and good cooking. She had enjoyed being out on the land with her father, helping him to mend fences and with other practical tasks that needed to be undertaken through the winter months. She had returned to her rooms in Boston just after the New Year, where she had hoped that there might be a response from Mr. Jenks. Her heart had sunk when there was still no reply from him, despite having had a further two letters from Mr. Thompson and one from the town council of Copperton Mill.

She wasn't sure why, but it rather hurt that Mr. Jenks had not replied to her in so long. His letter to her had seemed so eager. Maybe her telling him of the trials facing her in finding work and how hard it was to be a woman in a man's domain had been too much, and he had decided that he did not wish for such an independent-minded woman after all. Perhaps her letter had gone missing in the post, but she had also sent him Season's Greetings, wishing him a Merry Christmas and a very happy and healthy New Year. Both letters could not possibly have gone missing, could they?

Well, it was best not to dwell upon it, so she sat down to carefully craft her responses to Copperton Mill and Mr. Thompson. Both wished to meet her, and Copperton Mill had even sent her rail tickets so she might visit the town. Mr. Thompson had said that he would be happy to come to Boston, or perhaps meet her in Chicago so neither of them had as far to travel, and they could meet on neutral territory, so to speak. Anna couldn't help thinking that would be an excellent idea, and she wondered if the town council might agree to something similar. If she liked them, she could continue and visit the town. If she did not, she could go home or remain in Chicago while she decided what to do next.

With her mind made up, she wrote her responses and hurried to the postal office to mail them. Snow had been falling all day, and it was so cold she could see every puff of breath as she walked briskly, rubbing her hands to try to keep them warm even through the thick gloves her parents had given her for Christmas.

Shivering, she let herself back into the house and bumped into Mrs. Phelps in the hallway. "I see it's not letting up," the older woman said, nodding at the flakes of snow encrusting Anna's golden hair and on her coat.

"No, I think it's getting worse," Anna agreed. "We'll be trapped indoors soon if it carries on this way."

"I've plenty of food in the pantry," Mrs. Phelps assured her. "Nobody here will starve if that happens. My son William said we'd be in for a hard winter this year, so I've been putting a little something away every week since September, just in case."

"Let us hope it will not be needed," Anna said. This was the moment to tell her, but suddenly it seemed too hard to do so. Mrs. Phelps had been so much more than a landlady to her; she was a friend—one so close that she was almost family.

"Would you like to join me in the parlor for some hot chocolate?" Mrs. Phelps asked, a naughty grin on her face as if doing such a thing in the mid-afternoon was quite unseemly. "I know I normally only have it at breakfast, but in this weather, you want something warm and sweet to perk you up, I think."

"That sounds lovely," Anna said. She took off her coat and hung it carefully on the hooks by the door where it could dry out and not get anyone else's wet. "We deserve a treat. I quite agree that this kind of weather can make one miserable."

"Well, the doctor has ordered it, so I must obey," Mrs. Phelps said, giggling. "I shall fetch some of my chocolate cake, too. I know how much you like it."

Anna settled into a chair by the fire and waited for Mrs. Phelps to return. She had learned over the years not to offer to help. Mrs. Phelps liked to spoil her, and Anna was sure the older woman looked upon her as the daughter she'd never had. She stared at the oil painting above the mantel for a moment. It was a seascape featuring the ship that Mr. Phelps had served on during his time in the Navy. The boat was being tossed around in a storm, the waves ferocious, the dark clouds menacing. It must have been a perilous life indeed to put to sea, Anna often thought. Before long, Mrs. Phelps returned with a tray full of goodies.

"I've brought all sorts. I've not seen you for such a long time. We have much to catch up on. Firstly, you must tell me, how are your dear parents?"

"They are quite well, busy as always, and they send their very best regards," Anna said honestly.

"And was Christmas with them wonderful?"

"It was," Anna said with a wistful smile. "I got to see some of my old friends, my aunt and uncle, and my cousins. And of course, I spent a lot of time with Mom and Dad. They are still trying to buy that piece of land. Old Man Hull is being very tricky about it. I think they may give up and look elsewhere if he doesn't give them a good price soon. And stick to it."

"That would be a shame, and I know they were very excited that they finally had the funds to purchase it. Why are some old men so very difficult?" Mrs. Phelps said, shaking her head. "My father was the same as this Mr. Hull. Always changing his mind, contrary as can be. Drove everyone that had to do business with him half mad."

"I can imagine. I think Old Man Hull rather enjoys the attention. He's a lonely soul. He'll back down in time if he thinks Dad really will go elsewhere."

"I do hope so."

Anna watched Mrs. Phelps pour the thick chocolate from the beautiful silver pot, then took her cup and drank in its rich, sweet scent before taking a sip. It was delicious, warming, and soothing. Anna relaxed into her chair and just enjoyed the moment. She put her cup on the table beside her when Mrs. Phelps handed her a slice of cake, and the two were quiet for a moment as they ate it greedily. "You truly do make the finest cake in Boston, Mrs. Phelps."

"Thank you, and you are too kind. I do enjoy baking, though. I find it keeps my hands and mind busy when I don't want to think too much about other things."

"There is much to be said for that," Anna said, standing up momentarily to place her plate back on the tray. She took another sip of her chocolate as she tried to fortify herself to tell Mrs. Phelps that she would be leaving again and, this time, she might not be returning.

She took a deep breath. "Mrs. Phelps, I have some news."

"You do?" Mrs. Phelps' eyes lit up excitedly.

"Yes, I have been offered a position at last," Anna said.

"You do not look as happy as I had expected you to be when you came to me with such news."

"That is because I have a few concerns about it. The first is that I would be the only doctor in a new practice. That is a little daunting for someone who has barely left medical school."

"I can understand that," Mrs. Phelps said, nodding sagely. "You're a good doctor, though. Look at all the experience you've had treating everyone who stays here and at the hospital. And I am sure Dr. Skallin will not mind you asking his advice if you need it."

"That is where the second concern comes in. It is in a town called Copperton Mill in South Dakota," Anna said. She bit her lip as she waited nervously for her landlady's response to the news.

"Ah," Mrs. Phelps said after a lengthy pause. "I see."

"I have not said yes," Anna assured her. "At least, not yet. But I am considering it because it would be an excellent opportunity for me, and I am not exactly fending off offers from anywhere else. They sent me tickets to go and visit the town, but I am unsure that I wish to travel all that way only to find I don't like them or that things are not as they have promised me."

"I think you are wise to trust your instincts, Anna. Perhaps meet them here or in Chicago. I have a dear friend who runs a boarding house there. I could write to her and have her keep you a room if you'd like?"

"Oh, would you do that?" Anna said, surprised at how well the older woman was taking her news. "That would be quite wonderful. I had thought that might be the best solution, but with nowhere to stay and no idea where to start to find a place, I was quite at a loss."

"Ellspeth Havermeier has long owed me a favor—one I thought I would probably never need to ask her to repay. She will be glad to put you up. And I'll keep your room here. You will always be welcome if you come back to visit your family." Mrs. Phelps looked like she might cry, and Anna was struggling to hold back tears herself. Her kindness was so generously given, with no thought of return for herself.

"I was so lucky when I came to live here," Anna said, getting up and moving across the room to hug Mrs. Phelps. "You have been like an aunt, or if I did not already have such a wonderful one, a mother. I cannot thank you enough for all the little kindnesses you have shown me over the years, all the support and concern. I will never forget you, whatever happens to me."

"You will make a success of whatever you try. That is who you are. Just be careful out there." Her expression was haunted, even a little sad, as she continued speaking, with a tone somber and serious. "Sometimes, it is better to admit defeat and leave before you break yourself chasing after success."

Anna nodded, but she wasn't entirely sure that she understood the warning in those words. She hugged Mrs. Phelps again, then remembered that she hadn't told her about her search for a husband. She told her about Mr. Thompson and his wish to meet her, and about the lost opportunity with Mr. Jenks and how much it had upset her. Mrs. Phelps looked amused.

"Well, you have been setting yourself up for an adventure, but adventures also bring heartache from time to time," she said gently.

"Oh, I know," Anna said. "I am hoping and praying that my years of having to fight for everything so hard will be behind me once I find a position and a husband, though I know there will always be struggles along the way. I fear I am almost out of fight after everything I have already faced.

"You'll know when it is right," Mrs. Phelps said, nodding her head and smiling. "And I hope that all these troubles will soon be behind you, too."

She cut another slice of cake and handed it to Anna, then another for herself before she continued to speak. "I know it may seem hard to imagine me as a young woman, but I felt the same way you do about your Mr. Jenks when I first met my husband. There was something about him from the first, though I could not have put my finger on it had you asked. I just knew he was the one for me. Perhaps there is still time for you to hear from this Mr. Jenks. I will send any letters that come here for you to Mrs. Havermeier. If he writes again, you'll know soon enough."

CHAPTER 8

January 1880, Iron Creek, Minnesota

The snow had been falling for what felt like an eternity. Most of the town was snowed in, though Alec and a few of the farmers had tried to clear some of the roads. They'd kept them clear long enough to check that everyone in town had enough to eat until the snow thawed, then had to accept that the only place to be warm and cozy was inside their homes until the worst passed. Alec hated being cooped up. He wasn't the kind of man content just sitting by the fire, reading or whittling. He needed to be busy.

Deciding that all the inactivity would soon drive him crazy, he decided to undertake some tasks around the house. The attic hadn't been cleared out in way too long, and he was sure there were things up there that could be reused if he fixed them. Now was the perfect time to see if he could make those repairs. He fetched the few tools he had in the house, checked them over to make sure they were fit, and then, every morning for three days, he made his way up the rickety ladder into the attic space and lit a couple of lamps so he could see what he was doing in the gloom. He sorted through the piles of junk that had been shoved up there, out of the way, and soon had three piles. The first was of things that were too broken to ever be of any use to anyone, the second held the items he was sure he could mend, and the third was of the things he wished to keep but had no place in the house right then. He tidied those away and took the rest downstairs.

He piled the things with no purpose high on the back porch, ready to load into the wagon so he could dispose of them when the snow cleared. He was surprised at just how much had accumulated since he'd moved to Iron Creek. He'd obviously fallen into bad habits, just shoving things up into the attic rather than mending them or throwing them away then and there. He vowed to be more attentive in the future and not to let things get so out of hand again.

He sorted the pile of broken things into an order of how easy they would be to fix. Some would need parts he would have to buy in Grand Marais or even Duluth. For others, he would need to make parts once he could reopen the forge. He put those items on the front porch in as neat a pile as he could. He was left with just a handful of items that he could do something with while stuck in the house, and he set about fixing them right away. By the time the snow began to melt, and he could get back to the forge, all of them had been fixed.

After almost ten days away from his forge, Alec was delighted when the snow finally began to melt. He walked along Main Street in the early hours of the morning while it was still dark and quiet, keen to light the fires. He whistled quietly to himself, glad to be outside, glad to be away from his mother after so long in such close quarters, and glad to be about to get back to what he loved best. Though it was still cold, he was as happy as he had ever been.

When he reached his shop, he went about his chores as he always did, lighting the fire and laying out his tools. It might take some time to get the forge back to the temperature he needed to work the metal, but he would tend the fire until it was as it should be, no matter how long it took. Breaks such as this one could cause all kinds of problems for him, thanks to the lost work during the bad weather and the time it took to get back up and running. He watched as the flames flicked higher, then slowly lower and lower. By midday, the fire was just a mass of glowing red and orange, and he began to work once more, bending and shaping iron, his skills coming back to him quickly after the forced time away.

A few customers stopped by to request items, and things were as back to normal as he could hope for by the end of the day. Alec had a full order book for the next few weeks. Though his arms and back ached a little as he headed home, he knew that by the morning, those minor bothers would be but mere memories as his muscles got used to the work again. He banked the fire and was about to head for home when he saw Nelson Gustavson bringing the stagecoach to a halt outside the postal office. Hank Wilson was waiting for him. Nelson handed him several large bags of letters and packages—a backlog caused by the snow, no doubt. Nelson clicked to his horses to move on while Hank took the bags into the postal office to sort through them.

The sight reminded Alec of the letters he'd received back in October, especially the letter from Dr. Macdonald. It still stung that she'd not replied, and he hated that he still felt as though he had missed out on an incredible opportunity. He had yet to place a new advertisement in the newspaper, though he knew that he would probably have to do so before long. Before the snows, he'd tried to convince himself that he'd do it soon, that there was no hurry, but in reality, he had been giving Dr. Macdonald time to change her mind and write to him again. It was probably time to accept that she wasn't going to.

He was about to close the gates and lock up when he saw a woman hurrying toward the postal office. She was bundled up against the cold, but Alec would have known her gait anywhere. It was Mama. He was about to call out to her, then changed his mind. Why would Mama be chasing down the stagecoach? Was she expecting visitors? Or perhaps a particular letter from someone? But who could she be expecting to receive a letter from that was so important that she couldn't wait until the morning, when Hank would deliver everyone's mail to their door?

He stood in the shadows and watched his mama enter the postal office and hurry out of it and back home as quickly as she had come. Alec shook his head, wondering what was going on. Such behavior was not normal, not even for Mama. As he waited, trying to make sense of it, he saw Hank lock up and head for his home, clearly not surprised by his mother's actions. That only made Alec think that it had happened before. But how many times before? And for how long?

With his mind a muddle of thoughts, Alec made his way home. He took off his boots before he reached the porch to avoid making a sound as he approached and crept inside on tiptoe. For such a big man, he could be exceptionally light on his feet when he wanted to be. He'd learned the skill as a boy, trying to creep out of the house at night to go and spend time with his friends. It was a skill that had served him well.

His mother was not in the kitchen when he entered. Nor was she in the parlor or the pantry. He guessed she must be upstairs. He made his way up the stairs, praying as he took each step that it wouldn't creak under his weight. He padded softly along the landing to his mother's bedroom. The door was open. Inside, his mother was hurriedly placing something into a box that she then shoved under her bed. She sat down on the bed, biting her lip a little, a look of fear in her eyes.

Alec had never known her to be so secretive. What could possibly be contained in those letters that made her look so afraid? Now was not the time to confront her, though. He vowed to find a way to read the letters so she need never know. If they contained something he didn't need to be concerned about, he would leave the matter to her. If there was anything he could do to help her, he would do it.

He backed away and crept back down the stairs before she came out onto the landing. He let himself out silently, pulled his boots back on, then tramped up onto the porch, and let himself inside as he normally did. Mama was at the stove as she always was. She kissed him as she always did. And she made no mention of her meeting with Hank Wilson or of the box of letters under her bed. Alec did his best to be nonchalant and went up to get washed and dressed for dinner. As he always did.

But, knowing she was busy at the stove and would not disturb him, he made his way straight to his mother's room and pulled out the box. He placed it on the bed and pulled out a handful of the letters inside. He flicked through them slowly. The stamps upon them told him they had come from all over the country, from New York, Rhode Island, Virginia, and Philadelphia. There were some from Utah, Mississippi, and Texas, and one from Florida. But most importantly, there were three letters from Boston—all in Dr. Macdonald's handwriting.

Alec sank down on the bed. He had thought that perhaps his mother had gotten into some kind of trouble. Perhaps there were debts of his father's or something she had not wished to share with him. That she had been keeping his letters from him had not once crossed his mind. Why would she do such a thing? Why would she interfere in his life in such a way?

The seals were already broken. He felt utterly betrayed. His mother had not only kept his mail from him, she had read it. But why? She should have been glad that he was looking for a wife. After all, she was constantly telling him to find one so she could have grandchildren. So then, why hide these letters? Why delay or disrupt his attempts to find the woman who might provide the babies Mama so often said she longed for?

He unfolded the first letter. It must have only been sent quite recently. Dr. Macdonald was telling him the news that she had been offered a position and that she was coming to Chicago to meet members of the town council of a place called Copperton Mill in South Dakota. He quickly opened the other two in her handwriting and found letters as charming and wonderful to him as the first one she'd sent all those months ago. As he read them, he grew even angrier. Not only had his mother interfered with his life, but she had made this clever, determined young woman doubt herself. She was clearly very hurt that he had not written, yet she was prepared to make excuses for him, that perhaps all her letters had gotten lost along the route. Mixed in with his rage toward his mother, it struck him that Dr. Macdonald had continued to write to him even though he had not responded to her two previous letters. He couldn't help hoping that he wouldn't be too late to write to her now.

He looked back at the most recent letter and the date upon it. If his reckoning was correct, she would be arriving in Chicago during the first week of February. He could be there, too. He could write to her, he knew that, and that would be by far the easiest course of action. But after what had happened, he felt he owed it to her to be there in person, to explain and beg her forgiveness. She deserved an explanation, and he knew, deep down inside his very soul, that he needed to meet her. He needed to know he had done all he could to make it up to her.

Except for the rare times that they'd been snowed in, and those horrible weeks when he had stayed with Mama until Papa's funeral was over, Alec had never closed the forge since he'd moved to Iron Creek. He would close it now. This was the most important thing to him right then. More important than his work or his mother's happiness. More important than anything.

He had been sure from the first moment he'd seen Dr. Macdonald's handwriting that she was the woman for him. Her forthright manner and straightforward way of expressing herself had endeared her to him in a way no small talk ever could. After reading some of the other replies from women all over the country, he had been certain that there was nobody else he wanted. She was everything he could imagine ever wanting, and he did not care one bit whether his mother approved or not.

Alec put the letters back into the box and took it downstairs to the kitchen, keeping it hidden behind his back. "Oh good," his mother said without turning around. "You're here. Everything is just perfect. Take a seat, darling."

She turned with a tureen of buttered potatoes in her hands. "Why are you not washed and changed?" she asked, placing it on the table.

Alec set the box down and waited for her explanation. She blanched, her mouth dropping wide open, her eyes even wider. "Where did you get that?" she spluttered. "What were you doing in my room?"

"I should think that is obvious," he said. "I saw you, Mama, chasing after the stagecoach, fetching our mail from Hank. You've been keeping these from me. And what is worse, you have been reading letters that were meant only for me. How could you do that?"

His mother's skin changed from white to red as she stared at him, for once unable to find anything to say. Alec sat down and pushed the box toward her. "Sit, Mama," he said. "Tell me everything from the start."

His mother wrung her hands nervously and licked her parched lips. "I opened the first one by accident," she said, her tone panicked, desperate for him to believe her. "I truly didn't mean to. I didn't even check the address. You so rarely get mail, and I know that Hank usually brings you anything important to the forge. I'd just come back from Chicago, and you were working such long hours."

"That isn't an excuse, Mama."

"I know. I should have given it to you. I should never have read it once I realized it was not for me."

"So, why did you?"

"I couldn't help it. That woman sounded so dreadful. Everything was all about her and how clever she was to have become a doctor and how she didn't want to be a wife and mother. Yet she was writing to you, like the others were, because of an advertisement you had placed for just that. It didn't seem right to me, a woman to be so, so..." she trailed off, unable to finish her thought.

"So modern? So independent? So intelligent? So determined?" Alec asked.

"Alec, don't make me say something I'll regret," his mother pleaded. "I am sorry for what I have done. Can we not just leave it at that?"

"No. You've just insulted a woman you know nothing about. Can you not for one minute imagine how difficult it must have been for a woman, any woman, to get accepted into medical school, to become a doctor, when even other women would make her feel bad for wanting to even try? You, who knows how hard it was for Papa, who had all the privileges his family and his sex could give him?"

His mother nodded, looking chagrined. "I am sorry. And she is to be admired for that, I suppose," she said grudgingly. "But if you are looking for a wife, she is hardly the type to make a good one."

"And what would you know of what I might wish for in a

wife?" he asked. "After all, I do not need anyone to keep house for me, do I? What would a wife do if I were to force her to remain at home simply twiddling her thumbs all day?"

The pair glared at each other. Alec had never been so angry with anyone in his entire life. "I am going to Chicago," he announced, standing up from the table and pushing his chair away with a loud scraping noise. "I intend to meet with her, and I will apologize to her for your misguided actions. While I am gone, I expect you to write to every one of these women to apologize to them, too." His mother made to speak, but Alec had heard enough. He raised his hand and frowned at her. "I will hear no argument."

He walked out of the house, saddled up his horse, and rode up to Garrett and Katy Harding's place, where he knew he would get a warm welcome, a good meal, and a comfortable bed for the night. Alec couldn't bear the thought of even being close to his mother right then. Once he'd had a chance to get a bed set up, he would sleep in the barn at the forge. He would get some of his things from the house when Mama went to the store. He had much to do before he could leave for Chicago, including finding someone to mind the forge while he was gone. He didn't need to shut it, he realized, but the decision depended on finding the right person to look over it in his absence. But even if he was unable to find someone, he would close everything down and go anyway. He owed it to Dr. Macdonald to explain everything. He prayed she would forgive him.

Something his mother had said to him just a few days ago gave him another idea. Whether Dr. Lancelot would be free to go to Chicago with him at such short notice might be a different matter, but he had to try. He was so sure that Dr. Macdonald was the woman he was supposed to meet. For them to have a chance to make up their minds about each other, she needed to find a position as a doctor as close to Iron Creek as he could find one.

CHAPTER 9

February 1880, Chicago, Illinois

Travel was exhausting and extremely dull after the first hundred miles or so. Despite the ever-changing scenery, Anna had had more than enough of it by the time she finally reached Chicago. When she got to the boarding house that Mrs. Phelps had recommended, Mrs. Havermeier greeted her with warmth and affection, a bath in front of the fire in her room, and a hot meal. Once settled into her new accommodations, Anna started to explore the city. It was busy, with lots of people rushing here and there, like Boston—but in every other way, it was completely different.

Things seemed much less refined. People dressed less formally, for a start. Most of the men wore denim pants, plaid shirts, and vests that denoted them as cowboys. Though there were a few men in tailored suits around, it was clear that men of the professions were in the minority. Women mostly wore simple dresses, usually in gingham or floral fabrics, though again there were a few who were obviously wealthier—the wives and daughters of the well-dressed bankers, doctors, and lawyers who kept up with the Eastern fashions.

There were markets everywhere, selling everything from livestock to furniture, fruits and vegetables to fabrics and knick-knacks. Everything seemed louder, and people often yelled at one another from one end of the street to the other or spoke in raised voices so they could be heard over the general hubbub. Even in the poorest areas of Boston, Anna could not recall such informality or such a wall of noise.

Despite all that—or perhaps because of it—she loved the city's vibrancy. It was clear that everyone there was an adventurer. Even those clad in elegant suits and gowns had that pioneering spirit; they might have dull occupations, but they had taken the risk to come west and to make their fortune. Most of the people Anna met had either come to Chicago some years earlier to have an adventure or were passing through on their way further west to start a new one. Even those born in the city seemed to have an air that anything was possible about them. Nobody seemed to think anyone's hopes and dreams were too outrageous to be made real.

The delegation from Copperton Mill was due to join her the next day. Anna was in equal measures excited and anxious about meeting with them. It was the only real option she had to continue in her career, so the meeting was laden with importance for her. She knew that she could not make any errors. She had to impress them and show them that she was up to the task—and she would do just that.

She knew that a first impression was sometimes all anyone paid attention to, so she had planned every element of her meeting with them to the best of her ability. Now she had to hurry to the Chinese laundry at the end of the street to fetch her best dress. She'd taken it to them on Mrs. Havermeier's recommendation. She had been surprised at the number of Chinese people in the city. Many had come to America, like many people from all over the world had, to try to strike it lucky in the numerous gold rushes. Some had gone home again; others had stayed.

The kindly Chinese lady who had taken her gown a few days ago beamed at her as she entered the shop. Then she started speaking a torrent of rapid-fire Mandarin to one of the men behind her, who disappeared for a moment and returned with Anna's blue velvet dress, perfectly cleaned and pressed. Anna smiled as she saw how beautifully they had taken care of it and handed over the money required for their care and attention.

She took the gown back to Mrs. Havermeier's boarding house and was just letting herself in through the front door of the three-story townhouse when the rusty-haired lad from the postal office bounded up the steps behind her. "Plenty of letters for you today, miss," he said with a sassy grin as he leafed through the bundle in his hand. "And you've barely been here a week. Must be nice to be popular and know people in so many places." He grinned, causing his cheeks to dimple. Somehow, it made his freckles stand out even more, too.

Anna was only expecting letters from Mr. Thompson and the Copperton Mill town council, so she was surprised when she found that there was also a letter from a Dr. Lancelot, who came from Iron Creek, Minnesota. It seemed a rather unkind coincidence that she should receive anything from that town, given she had still not heard anything from Mr. Jenks.

She went inside and took her letters upstairs, leaving those for Mrs. Havermeier and the rest of the guests on the hallway table. As she climbed the stairs, she tried to recall applying for a position in Minnesota, and more particularly Iron Creek, but could not. She had applied to many small towns all over the country, but she would have remembered the coincidence of contacting a man to be his wife and applying for a position in the same town. Yet, she could think of no other reason for a doctor from such a small town to contact her. She had no family in Minnesota and knew nobody there at all other than Mr. Jenks, and he was a tentative acquaintance at best.

Yanking off her coat hurriedly, the letters held between her teeth, Anna almost tumbled over. She quickly laid her coat and newly laundered dress onto the bed and settled down on the chair at the little table by the window without taking off her boots. With her letter opener, she quickly sliced the seal of Dr. Lancelot's letter. His writing was hurried, a looping scrawl that was hard to read, as so many doctors' handwriting seemed to be. Anna slowly managed to get used to it and decipher the message within.

Dear Dr. Macdonald,

It has been brought to my attention that you may be searching for a suitable position, having recently completed your medical studies and training at Harvard. I must confess that I did not attend such a hallowed school myself, but I have had a successful practice in and around the communities near Devil Track Lake for over forty-five years.

The town of Iron Creek is growing rapidly, and I find myself spending most of my time there. This means that the more remote communities are no longer as well served, as I simply do not have the time or the energy to attend them as much as I would like. And it means that people I care for are going untreated because either I cannot get to them, or they cannot get to me.

However, the growth in the population of the town means that I am in a position to take on additional staff and have a need for another doctor to serve the smaller and more far-flung communities that fall under my care. To begin with, the position might not offer as much work as you might prefer. It can take some time for the local people to come to trust and put their faith in any doctor, and—I hope you do not mind me saying this—a lady doctor will find this even harder, I fear.

However, if you are willing to consider such an arrangement, I would be glad to meet with you. I will be in Chicago on the day of the twentieth of February if that might suit you? If it does, please send word to me at the Grand Pacific Hotel.

Yours most cordially,

Dr. Andrew Lancelot

Anna shook her head and re-read this letter that had come out of nowhere, wondering if someone was playing a cruel game with her. It was already the twenty-first of February. What if Dr. Lancelot had already left town? What if he thought she was not interested? She grabbed her coat from where she'd left it on the bed and hurried down the stairs and onto the street.

She grabbed one of the messenger boys as he passed by. "Which way to the Grand Pacific Hotel?," she demanded of him. He gave her a slightly scared look, but pointed to her left, then gave her a hurried list of instructions on how to get to the grand palazzo-style building on the block bounded by Clark Street, LaSalle, Quincy, and Jackson. Anna thanked him and gave him a penny for his troubles before running the entire way.

She was red-faced and out of breath when she arrived fifteen minutes later. The hotel was very fancy, even more so in some ways than the Crawford Rooms back in Boston. Anna could hardly stop herself from staring at the immaculate floors, the grand columns, and the beautiful ceiling as she made her way across the lobby to a gleaming mahogany desk, where a liveried man stood poring over a large ledger.

"Excuse me," Anna said, with a polite cough to get his

attention. "I wonder if you might help me. I was hoping to meet with Dr. Andrew Lancelot, but I may have missed him due to a delay in receiving his letter. He was to stay with you yesterday, I believe." She showed him the letter to prove that she had, in fact, been invited by the doctor himself.

The man nodded, with an impassive face. "Please wait here," he said, pointing her toward an elegantly carved chair, upholstered with red velvet and gold trim a yard from the desk. She sat down and watched him move smoothly and swiftly away from her. He soon disappeared into one of the rooms that led off from the vast foyer. Anna fidgeted in her seat. She was a little too warm, but the dress she was wearing beneath her coat was not one she wished to meet a future employer in—if Dr. Lancelot was indeed still here. She caught a glimpse of her reflection in a mirror on the wall nearby. So much for making a good first impression. Her hair had come unpinned, and her skin was a little blotchy still from her exertions. Anxiously, she tried to fix her hair as best she could without a brush or comb, then pinched her cheeks to try to at least make the redness a little more uniform.

A few moments later, the somewhat haughty concierge reappeared. Behind him were two men. One was tall and heavily muscled, with a handsome face and sandy hair that he wore just a little too long. He was clad in the new denim trousers so favored by cowboys and a smart white cotton shirt, which though on any other man would have been quite loose, strained a little as it passed over his broad chest and muscular arms. He wore it with a shoe-string tie and a dark gray vest. He towered over his companion. As they drew closer, Anna was sure that she could fit both her hands into one of his.

The second man was short and plump and had the whitest hair Anna had ever seen. He had a jovial expression. Anna was sure that this must be Dr. Lancelot. She stood up, and the older man beamed at her and shook her hand enthusiastically as he introduced himself. It made Anna smile. He was the first doctor to treat her as an equal, other than dear Dr. Skallin. "I am so delighted that you are here," he gushed. "Mr. Connor told us of your predicament, that the letter only arrived today. I had so hoped it would get here before we did. That is something that you learn when you live in these parts. The mail can never entirely be trusted to arrive when you want it to."

"So it would seem," Anna said, amused by his kindly manner and patient temperament. He indicated that they should all sit and asked Mr. Connor to bring them some tea.

"And, of course, you know Mr. Jenks," he said swiftly, almost glossing over it and certainly not giving Anna time to contradict him. "He speaks very highly of you indeed, and he's a man I trust implicitly."

Anna looked over at the taller, younger man. So, this was Mr. Jenks? At first glance, she had been right to think he was the most interesting of the men she had written to in the hope of finding a husband. Having met Mr. Thompson just the day before, it was clear which of them had the greater physical appeal. Mr. Thompson was sweet and polite and had excellent manners, but there was something forced about him. It was as if his behavior did not come entirely naturally to him. He had been perfectly dressed, too, yet did not look comfortable in his attire.

This man, however, was clearly at peace with himself. He wore his clothes well, though they were not tailored or at the very height of fashion. They suited him, as did the calluses on his hands and the amused look in his gray eyes. "I am grateful to Mr. Jenks," she said, tearing her eyes away and doing all in her power to keep her attention solely on Dr. Lancelot. "He is too kind to sing my praises without telling me he intended to do so. I have not heard from him in many months."

She glanced back at Mr. Jenks, who had the decency to flinch at the intended slight. Dr. Lancelot either ignored the slight tension between them or did not notice it at all. He blithely continued to look at her closely, as if trying to take her full measure with his eyes. "I told you almost everything regarding the position in my letter, I believe. If you have any questions, I would be happy to answer them," he said, looking at her intently.

Anna hadn't had time to even consider such a thing, but she had been preparing to speak with the town council, so the questions she had prepared to ask them were fresh in her mind. She asked them one by one, noting Dr. Lancelot's answers carefully and comparing them to what she knew of the position with the council. Dr. Lancelot compared very favorably, and Anna felt herself warming to this kindly and gentle man. He would make a wonderful mentor in the next stage of her medical education and training.

From time to time, she glanced over at Mr. Jenks. He looked slightly uncomfortable in the chairs that were perfectly comfortable if you were the size of a woman or a man like Dr. Lancelot. Mr. Jenks was built in the image of a bear, with all the animal's latent strength but more than any man's fair share of good looks. His features were so perfectly cut, they were as if chiseled from stone by an artist of the highest caliber. He was out of place in this setting, but Anna couldn't help thinking that he must be quite magnificent in his forge.

"Now, I'm afraid I must go. I have to catch the stagecoach back to Iron Creek this afternoon, so if you will excuse me, Dr. Macdonald, I must leave you," Dr. Lancelot said, standing up. She followed suit. Again, he shook her hand like an equal. "I should be delighted if you decide to join me, but I understand that you do have another potential position to consider. Take your time to choose. It is important that you choose the right one for you."

With that, he bowed and left them, bounding up the nearby grand staircase with the energy of a much younger and much slighter man. "Thank you," Anna said, turning to Mr. Jenks. "Though I must confess to being more than a little confused."

CHAPTER 10

February 1880, Chicago, Illinois

Alec had watched Dr. Anna Macdonald closely as she and Dr. Lancelot spoke. She was charming. And she was so impassioned when she spoke of her work, as he had expected her to be. Yet, she still maintained a calm and approachable demeanor, much as Dr. Lancelot did. They seemed to be getting on as well as he could possibly have hoped, and that made his heart lift just a little.

His emotions had been somewhat erratic since finding out that his mother had kept all of his letters from him for months. His anger ebbed and flowed, and though his brain attempted to give his mother excuses for such behavior, he could not bring himself to accept any of them—at least, not yet. She had betrayed his trust. She had interfered in his personal life in a way that currently felt unforgivable.

Yet, all was not entirely lost. Dr. Macdonald was there, sitting right in front of him, looking even more perfect than he could ever have imagined. Her curly blonde hair was pinned in the fashionable way women wore it in Boston, and her blue wool coat was cut to the shape of her body, emphasizing her curves and her sable-lashed, blue eyes. She was what any man would call pretty, yet her fierce independence and passionate discourse made her so much more than that. He found her mesmerizing.

But now it was time to explain himself, and he simply did not have the words. Telling her the truth seemed so silly. That a grown man might have his post stolen by his mother seemed ludicrous, and he so wished to impress her. He knew that she was honest, to the point of being blunt if necessary, so nothing but the truth would do. She would see through any lie, no matter how tiny; he was certain of that.

"I have much to tell you," Alec admitted. "And you have every right to be angry with me. If you are only confused, well, that is more than I possibly deserve."

"So, explain it to me," she said simply, leaning back a little in her chair and folding her hands in her lap. They were so small, so pale, and so elegant that Alec found himself distracted again.

He shook his head almost imperceptibly and took a deep breath. "This will sound quite nonsensical, but I swear to you that every word of it is true."

"I will wait and reserve judgment until you have finished, then," Dr. Macdonald said with a hint of a smile.

Alec told her of his happiness at receiving her letter and how eagerly he had responded to her. He had looked forward to receiving another letter for weeks, but nothing had come. Then a month had passed, then two, and he had assumed that she must no longer be interested in their correspondence.

"But I did write to you," she said, her tone insistent.

He nodded. "I know you did." He pulled out the small collection of her letters that he always kept with him now. "That was how I was able to give Dr. Lancelot your address here in Chicago to write you. But I only received your letters a little over a week ago."

"I don't understand," Dr. Macdonald said, looking perplexed. She looked too sweet, with her rumpled brow and the way she bit her lip a little when she was thinking hard.

"Believe me, neither do I. But I do have an explanation. One night, I was working in the forge late. It is not uncommon, as I have told you." He paused to take a breath. "When I closed up and got ready to go home, the stagecoach passed by the gates. I thought nothing of it. Nelson comes by at least once a week at that time. But it was after that, as I headed out onto the street to go home, that things became interesting."

"In what way?"

Dr. Macdonald was now leaning forward a little as if she was intrigued by what he might say next. Alec knew he wasn't a great storyteller, but this one seemed to need little assistance to be of interest. "My mother was hurrying to the postal office."

"Your mother? Was she expecting something?"

"It turns out she has been chasing down the stagecoach every time it comes through town to reach the mail before it reaches me," Alec said bluntly. "I found a stash of letters, mostly replies to my advertisement—and your letters—under my mother's bed."

"Oh my," Dr. Macdonald said, her eyes wide. "I cannot imagine such a thing. My parents would never dream of keeping my mail from me. Why would she do that?"

"I do not know. I have my suspicions, but I was so angry I left the house that night without truly trying to understand her motivations. I assume it was because she does not wish to share me. Since my father died, she has gotten used to taking care of my home and ensuring I am fed well. Perhaps the thought of another woman coming into my life that might supplant her was too much for her to bear."

Alec waited for her to react. She seemed surprised but not angry. Then, unexpectedly, she laughed. It echoed a little in the large foyer, making a few people nearby turn and stare. She stifled her amusement and gave him an understanding look. "I'm sorry," she said. "I know that I should not laugh. It isn't really funny. At Harvard, I saw many mother hens. So many of them smothered their sons, and I pitied any woman who might have to marry those poor men someday. They would have no say over anything in their own households."

"I fear that my mother may well be one of them, though I had never thought it possible before now. She has always encouraged me to marry and to have children before. It seemed so out of character." He gave a wry chuckle. "When I think of her, all bundled up running along Main Street like that…" he trailed off and laughed.

Dr. Macdonald laughed with him, and it was as if there had never been an issue to cloud their friendship. They seemed to be able to pick up from where those first letters had left off. Dr. Macdonald thanked him for speaking to Dr. Lancelot on her behalf, and she told him about meeting Mr. Thompson. Alec had to keep himself under control as she did so, as he felt a fit of raw and powerful jealousy that another man might win her heart.

She did not seem to be overly enthusiastic about him, though, and they parted with a promise to see each other again the next day. Alec went up to his room, hopeful that he at least still stood a chance to win her, and that was something he wanted more than ever now that he had met her in person. Anna was everything she had seemed in her letters. Everything he had ever hoped for. And more. He could hardly wait until the next day when he would take her to the park so they could walk and talk some more.

After a restless night, Alec rose early, as he always did. He enjoyed coffee and a sumptuous breakfast in the breakfast room downstairs, then took a leisurely walk through the Chicago streets. He did not often stray far from the hotel or the markets when he came here normally, and that was rare enough. Alec made his way to the area of the city where the blacksmiths plied their trade. He watched as his fellow craftsmen worked their fires and the metal and chatted briefly with some of them as he passed by their forges.

One was using a technique that Alec had not seen before, so he asked the man about it. Over two hours had passed before he realized, and he made his apologies to the man, begging him to allow him to return the next day to learn more. He had to meet Dr. Macdonald and was at risk of being late. The man grinned at him and said he was most welcome; anyone with Alec's skills who was willing to work for free would always be welcome at his forge.

When Alec reached her boarding house, Dr. Macdonald was standing upon the stoop. She was wearing a pretty bonnet and her blue coat, with her cheeks rosy from the chill in the air. "I am sorry," he said, anguished about being late.

"You need not be," she said, pulling out a pocket watch from her handbag and studying it. "You are five minutes early. I was merely enjoying the winter sunshine. After all that time traveling in a dingy carriage, I have tried to spend as much of my time as I can outside in the fresh air. I believe it is excellent for the constitution."

He offered her his arm, and she tucked her tiny, leather-gloved hand through it. As they walked slowly along the street, their conversation covered all manner of subjects, from the benefits of fresh air and a daily walk to the morning Alec had enjoyed at the nearby forge. Dr. Macdonald smiled at his boyish passion as he told her of the opportunity he'd had to learn something new.

As they entered the park, a small dog, his coat dirty and matted, shot past them. He was followed by a small gang of boys with sticks. Some were throwing them at the little dog, while others were threatening to beat the poor animal when they caught up to it. Dr. Macdonald frowned. "I do so hate to see animals treated that way."

"I can put a stop to it for good if you would like me to," Alec said, knowing that as little as a stern look from a man like him would be more than enough to have a group of street children quaking in their boots.

Dr. Macdonald nodded. "I shall try to catch the poor dog and calm him if I can."

The two of them chased after the little band of troublemakers. In no time, Alec's long legs had caught up to them, and he grabbed the collar of the biggest lad. He knew all too well that you had to tackle the leader of a gang like this to get what you wanted from all of them. He nodded to Dr. Macdonald as she hurried past them, and she gave him a determined look as she headed into the bushes after the dog.

"What, precisely, is it that you think you're doing?" Alec said, with his deep voice booming. "What has that animal done to you to deserve such treatment? Would you like it if I chased you through the park with sticks, threatening to beat you and throwing things at you?"

When he had first been collared, the ringleader had tried to yank himself away. But when he looked up at the man who held him tight, he suddenly stopped struggling, his furious eyes grew contrite, and he hung his head. "We didn't mean no harm," he protested, but his voice was not as firm as he might have liked.

"Then why were you throwing sticks and threatening to beat that dog? Because both would definitely harm him."

The lad stared down at the ground. His friends dithered, unable to decide without his leadership whether they should run away or stay their ground. Dr. Macdonald emerged from the bushes, the small, honey-colored dog in her arms. Up close, Alec could see that the poor mite was shaking from top to toe, his big brown eyes wide with fear, but he seemed to know that Dr. Macdonald meant him no harm and snuggled in closer to her as they drew nearer to his tormentors.

Alec let go of the lad's collar. The boy jumped away from him and scowled as he and his friends ran away as fast as they could. "Hopefully, they'll not be so cruel in the future," Alec said, ruffling the top of the little dog's head. "He's a kind of terrier, I think. Very loyal, sweet animals, and excellent for rats."

Dr. Macdonald laughed. "I wonder if he belongs to someone. He seems generally well cared for. Perhaps we could ask around the city, perhaps put up some posters—you know, like the one's the sheriffs use for wanted criminals?"

"I think that's an excellent idea. But what will we do with him until then? He can't come back to the hotel with me. Do you think your landlady would let him stay for a few days?"

She shrugged and hefted the dog's weight in her arms a little so she could look into its face. "I don't know, but how could she resist this little face?"

They set off, retracing their steps back to the boarding house. Mrs. Havermeier was in her parlor, enjoying a quiet cup of tea. She looked surprised to see Dr. Macdonald back so soon, and even more so when she saw Alec. She stood up, with her mouth wide open as she looked up at him. "My, aren't you tall?" she said, then giggled, realizing how rude such a comment must seem.

"My mama said I'd grown out of everything but the cloth from a wagon by the time I was ten," Alec said with a grin. He was used to people being taken aback at the sight of him. She seemed grateful that he had accepted her slip in manners and soon made up for it by offering the dog a home in her drying room, next to the kitchen.

"He can catch any rats that dare to come through, though I keep a clean house here, and earn his keep," she said. She took him from Dr. Macdonald and started petting him. He seemed quite content with her, as he had been with Dr. Macdonald, and Alec didn't doubt that he'd have the time of his life while being taken care of by them both.

"What'll we do with him if we can't find his owners?" Dr. Macdonald asked, looking at Mrs. Havermeier, then at Alec, her expression full of concern.

"We'll cross that bridge when we need to," Mrs. Havermeier assured her. "Let's not borrow troubles. We will try to find them first. And then, well, we'll see."

CHAPTER 11

*M*arch *1880, Chicago, Illinois*

The days passed. The little dog gained a name: Wilfred. With his sweet face and soulful eyes, he had easily worked his way into Anna's heart. Mrs. Havermeier was besotted, too. She'd gradually let him move from the drying room to the parlor for an hour after supper, then at any time that Anna was not in. Finally, she had given Anna permission to have him up in her room. Wilfred was well trained and never made a mess in the house. He had taken to sleeping on Anna's bed, and she didn't have the heart to push him off, especially as the nights could still be a little cold. But there had been no inquiries for him, and she and Mr. Jenks had walked all over the city, posting his description on walls and handing out handbills. It seemed Wilfred was all alone in the world.

What to do about that was not Anna's only quandary. She had grown very fond of the little furball and was tempted to take him with her wherever it was she might end up next. He would be good company for her, given she'd be starting afresh in a new place. But that would mean that she would need to make a decision—and soon—about which position to take. And which man she preferred.

In her heart, the answer was easy. She wanted to go to Iron Creek. She wanted to be near Mr. Jenks and work alongside Dr. Lancelot. It wasn't the most lucrative or the most secure option. Mr. Jenks had made no mention of marriage or whether he wanted her to move to his hometown, but it was the option that felt right. She had liked Dr. Lancelot from the very first meeting. Though he had not been able to stay in Chicago long, their one meeting had told her everything she'd needed to know.

Mr. Thompson had called on her every other day for two weeks before he had been forced to return home to his businesses. He had left her with a proposal and an avowal of his strong and honorable feelings toward her. The delegation from Copperton Mill had left Chicago after they had met with Anna three times. They had been very eager to have her become their physician, and Anna couldn't help wondering why that was. How many men had turned them down, and what were their reasons for doing so? But Copperton Mill was over a hundred miles from where Mr. Thompson lived, which made both propositions a little less appealing.

And then there was Mr. Jenks. Anna hated to admit it but meeting him had changed everything for her. His words had intrigued her. His attitude toward women taking such important roles in society as doctors, lawyers, and so forth was utterly modern and very supportive. He had not only made the effort to meet her once he'd found out about his mother hiding her letters, but he had also done all he could to find her a position. And he had closed his forge for almost a month now, just to spend time with her. But he had not made clear his intentions.

Did she dare take the risk of following her heart? If she did, she would at least have the work that she wanted most, even if Mr. Jenks decided that she was not the woman for him. But that did not make sense. If he didn't like her, why was he still there? Why had he closed his forge and shut it down for so long if he did not care for her? So, why had he not asked her to come back to Iron Creek with him? Why was he hesitant about making her his bride? If he did not make a decision soon, she would have to before her meager funds ran out. She needed to begin work and soon, so she needed to know where she was going to do that.

As they walked home from a musical they'd watched at the concert hall that evening, Anna decided that enough was enough. She needed an answer, and if he would not ask her, then she would ask him. She took a few deep breaths, then stopped in the middle of the sidewalk, just outside Mrs. Havermeier's boarding house. "Mr. Jenks, I cannot tell you how much I have enjoyed these past weeks, spending time with you and getting to know you better."

"I am glad," he said, interjecting before she'd finished. He was clearly delighted by her words, judging by the grin on his handsome face. "I have enjoyed it, too."

Anna shook her head. "Please," she said. "I need to say this, and it is hard enough, so please do not interrupt me."

He nodded his agreement, his smiling face suddenly solemn. "I'm sorry, do go on."

"As you know, I came here to meet the people I needed to, to inform the decisions that may impact the rest of my life. I have now done that, and I must make a decision. To go back to Boston and my parents' farm or to go to Copperton Mill and take up the position of town doctor there. Or, I might choose to be wed to Mr. Thompson, who proposed to me just before he left."

"Or you could choose Iron Creek," Mr. Jenks said softly.

"Or I could choose Iron Creek," Anna repeated, looking up into his beautiful gray eyes. She didn't dare finish what she needed to know. Did he want her to choose Dr. Lancelot? Did he want her to choose him?

"Dr. Macdonald…" he started tentatively, then hesitated.

"Call me Anna," she said. It sounded so strange to hear him use her formal title over and over as he did.

"Anna." He spoke the word like a caress, almost as if he were tiptoeing over the word to see how it felt. "I will not lie to you; I want you to choose Iron Creek. I want you to choose Dr. Lancelot. And more importantly, I want you to choose me. However…" he paused and took a deep breath. "I cannot ask you to marry me. At least, not yet."

"Not yet," Anna echoed. "What precisely does that mean, Mr. Jenks?"

"Alec," he corrected her with a rueful smile. "The longer I have been away, the more the situation with my mother has played upon my mind. I cannot, in all good conscience, ask you to be my bride until you know exactly what that would entail. That is why I would like you to take Dr. Lancelot's position, to come to Iron Creek, where we might have a longer courtship, and you might meet my mother."

Anna gave a wry chuckle. At least he wanted her to meet his mother. But though the man she knew here in Chicago was fun and fearless, the suggestion made her doubt that she knew the real Alec. Would she find that he was different when his mother was running his days once more? Was this strong man really a coward underneath it all? "Do you think she will dislike me so much?" she asked him.

"No, I think she will resent you and will try to push you away. Not because she dislikes you, but simply because she will not wish to tolerate what you represent," he explained. "I did not think my mother would do the kind of thing she did. I thought she would one day make a wonderful mother-in-law to whoever I was blessed enough to fall in love with and wed.

But I fear she would do all in her power to make any woman in my life want to turn away and run. She would try to make your life a misery. And so, though I wish I could so freely offer you marriage, as Mr. Thompson did, I cannot because I would not wish to ever see you unhappy."

"But surely her fear is that you would choose a wife that might supplant her in your life. I have no desire to do that. I do not wish to put her out on the streets or to even take over the management of your home. I will be too busy to care about the things she holds dear."

"And I think that she will come to see that if we take things slowly, and she gets to know you not as my wife, but as the town's new doctor," Alec said sadly.

It was clear he had given the matter a great deal of thought and that his conclusions disappointed him just as much as they did her. But he wasn't saying he didn't want her. He wasn't saying that he would never propose to her. It was a faint hope and not at all the definite answer to her questions that she had wanted. But was it enough? Anna did not know. She wanted to reach up, to kiss his full lips. Maybe then she'd be sure? But she could not do such a thing. It would be improper. Instead, she sighed loudly.

"Well, I suppose I have my answer," she said, turning to go up the steps and into the house. He caught her wrist and spun her back round to face him. They stared into each other's eyes. The world stood still. He was so close Anna could feel his breath on her cheek, and she wondered if he might kiss her. She closed her eyes and waited, praying he would. But instead, he let go of her hand and stepped away.

"Good night," he said. "I know my answer is not what you wanted of me, but believe me, there is nothing I would like more than to beg you to be my wife. But I will not do that. Not until you have met my mother. Not until you are sure you are prepared for how much she will fight for me. You have already fought so hard for everything you have earned in your life. You should not have to fight for this, but I think it may be inevitable that we would need to." He looked her in the eyes, his expression solemn. "The decision is yours. And whether you choose to come to Iron Creek to be with me or not, do not think you have to pass up the opportunity to work with Dr. Lancelot. I can bear it if you don't choose me, though I think it would break my heart to see you every day and know that you might never be mine."

Anna bid him good night again and let herself into the house. This time, he did not stop her. Wilfred met her at the bottom of the stairs, his little tail wagging so hard it made the whole of his body wiggle along with it. She picked him up and hugged him tightly. "So, Wilf, what do I do?" she asked him. "I feel no clearer on my decision than I did this afternoon, though I at least know now why Mr. Jenks—Alec—has not yet proposed."

The little dog yipped as if he understood every word and

was offering sympathy. Anna kissed the tip of his nose and smiled at him. "Well, at least one decision is easy. Would you like to come with me wherever I go?" He yipped again and licked her cheek. Anna laughed. "Then that is settled; you shall be by my side, wherever our next adventure might take us."

She had just turned to head up the stairs when Mrs. Havermeier appeared in the doorway of her parlor. She was wearing her nightgown and a thick velvet robe. "Did you have a wonderful evening?" she asked Anna.

"I did," Anna said. "The musical was delightful. If you have time, it is playing until the end of the week. I think you would love it."

"I may ask one of my girlfriends to go with me," the older woman said, searching Anna's face in the lamplight. "You seem a little troubled."

"I have to decide my future," Anna said. "But I am not sure which way to turn."

"Might I suggest a light supper of seedcake and hot chocolate to help you decide? I was just going to fetch some for myself." Mrs. Havermeier's solution to most things was something sweet and comforting. Anna couldn't help but agree with her. Perhaps it might help her to talk it over with someone else while enjoying something rich and decadent.

"That sounds perfect," Anna said. She took off her coat and followed Mrs. Havermeier into the kitchen. They fell into the routine that they had built over the weeks of her stay, with

Anna fetching the cake and chocolate and Mrs. Havermeier putting the milk and cream into a pan to warm on the stove. Anna cut the cake, and Mrs. Havermeier whisked the cocoa into the boiling milk before adding sugar then pouring it into large cups. The pair took seats on either side of the stove. Mrs. Havermeier opened the door of the stove so the heat from the fire would warm them both while Anna explained her dilemma.

"How do I choose?" Anna asked her.

"What is it you want?" the older woman said, getting to the very heart of it.

"I want to go to Iron Creek," Anna said, without a moment's hesitation. "I want to work with and learn from Dr. Lancelot. And I want to be Alec Jenks' wife one day."

"Then you have your answer, my dear," Mrs. Havermeier said. "The next thing to consider is whether you have the courage to take the risk that you might only get half of what you want."

Anna nodded and sipped her chocolate. "That is the part I don't know," she admitted. "I think I do, but how can I be sure? Mr. Jenks introduced me to Dr. Lancelot. How could I possibly remain in a position he arranged for me should things fall apart due to his mother's interference? Could I bear to stay in such a small town, knowing I would see him every day? Would he want me to?"

"I cannot answer that, and neither can you, until it happens."

"Then the decision is made," Anna said. "I have come this far. I have taken so many risks and have always fought for what I want. If I give up now, without a fight, I might regret it for the rest of my life. I shall go to Iron Creek, and whatever will be will be."

CHAPTER 12

April 1880, Iron Creek, Minnesota

It had not taken Anna long to create quite a stir in the little town of Iron Creek. Alec couldn't help smiling whenever he thought about how easily she had won over the hearts of the often ornery townsfolk. They'd been hesitant about telling their troubles to a lady doctor at first, but she had shown great patience and skill, and soon they were lining up to see her just as they would for Dr. Lancelot. Of course, there were a few in town who refused to see her no matter how much pain they might be in, just because she was a woman, but as Anna often said to him, there was no changing the minds of such people. You just had to let them be.

Alec loved having her nearby. She would call into the forge from time to time, and he would stop his work so they could enjoy a coffee together and a short chat before they both went about their busy days. If they were both free in the evening or on Sundays, they would go walking. Alec loved showing her the best paths down to the creek and up into the mountains. Their friendship only grew closer the more time they spent in each other's company. Though their busy lives made that difficult, they perhaps valued their time together more because of that.

Unfortunately, Alec's mother was one of those who had not yet warmed to Dr. Anna's charms. She was wary of a woman holding the role her husband had so cherished throughout his life. To her, a doctor was a man, and that was as it should be. Women did not have the temperament or the stomach for such a role, in her mind. A woman should be proud to be a wife and a mother; she should need nothing more than that to give her fulfillment and happiness in her life. It infuriated Alec and meant that they remained estranged, so he was still living in the barn at the forge.

A soft yip alerted him to Wilfred's presence in the yard. Alec peered out of the barn, and the little terrier rushed toward him, wagging himself delightedly. Alec picked him up and let the little dog cover his face with licks as Anna hurried into the yard after him, her face apologetic. "I'm so sorry," she said. "I was just visiting Mr. Barclay, and he saw the gates were open, and he was away."

"I don't mind," Alec said, grinning at her. "It means I get to see you." He ruffled the dog's head. "Both of you," he added, looking into Wilfred's big brown eyes. He was rewarded with another lick to his cheek.

Anna smiled up at him, and Alec felt his heart flutter. She truly was the loveliest-looking woman he'd ever laid eyes upon. "You are welcome here whenever you or Wilfred wish to come, though it might be safer if you keep him on a leash when nearby. A forge can be a very dangerous place."

"You're right, of course," Anna said. "He just loves to wander and greet everyone. I swear, he is a large part of the reason the townsfolk are happy to let me treat them. Almost everyone loves him."

"He's a lovable little scamp," Alec agreed. "I am so glad we rescued him and that you chose to keep him. He is besotted with you." *As am I,* he thought, though he dared not say it out loud.

"I bumped into your mother at the general store this morning," Anna said, her sunny expression suddenly disappearing and an uncharacteristic frown taking its place. "She snubbed me, as she so often does."

"I do not know what to do about her," Alec admitted. "She is so stubborn."

"She may never accept me, not even as a doctor, much less as a part of your life."

Alec nodded his agreement. He couldn't bear to say such a thing out loud, but with every passing day, he feared that might just be the truth of the matter. His mother showed no signs of changing her stance on the idea of Alec marrying

Anna or about Iron Creek having a lady doctor. Alec wasn't sure if they were connected. Perhaps his mother would have been more polite if Anna had come there without any attachment to him, but he wasn't entirely sure. And it mattered little even if that were the case.

The simple truth of the matter was that he wanted Anna to be his wife *and* a doctor. The two were inextricably linked. For him, that was part of her appeal. Her focus and dedication to something greater than herself and her constant search for more knowledge and better skills impressed him greatly. Her tenacity in facing all the obstacles to achieve everything she had, made him admire her, and her kindness and generosity to her patients made him love her.

Yet his mother refused to even meet with her. As far as Mama was concerned, Anna was something less than she should be, because a woman should not pursue a man's position. Alec could not see a way to change that, and that made things very difficult for him. He loved his mother. He never wanted to disappoint her or hurt her, yet he would do both if he chose to wed Anna. But if he chose not to marry the woman that he knew he loved, he would be miserable. It was quite the conundrum.

"You look deep in thought," Anna said, her eyes full of concern.

"I was just thinking about what it might take to get my mother to change her mind," Alec admitted.

"I fear I would need to save the entire town from destruction." She gave a wry smile, but Alec knew that the situation played as heavily upon her mind as it did on his own.

"Then perhaps we'd better come up with a plan to put it in peril?" he quipped.

Anna laughed and reached for Wilfred. Alec handed the little chap over and gave him a last fondle of his floppy ears. "I'd rather wait a while. I'm still a little fatigued from all my travels and the amount of work Dr. Lancelot has sent my way," she joked back.

"I'll hold off my plans for a devastating flood then," he promised her.

He watched as she left the yard. She turned and gave him a little wave at the gates, then vanished along Main Street. Alec smiled to himself as he went about his work. He had a wagon to mend for Judd Barclay; without it, the man couldn't ensure the town had the supplies it needed. As always, as he worked, Alec found his fears and anxieties melting away. He was focused on his task and lost in the rhythm of the work. It helped to have at least some time in the day when he didn't have to be concerned about how to reconcile the troubles between himself and his mother. But it was all too close when each night he lay down on his trundle bed, with his long limbs hanging over the edges as he tried to get comfortable.

Dusk was falling while Alec continued to work. Suddenly, he heard a loud scream from somewhere out on Main Street. He dropped his hammer and ran out of the yard, looking left and right to see who it was. He could see nothing. Alec ran to the left, toward the postal office and the general store, peering down every side-alley as he did so. He didn't see anything. Then there was another scream and a pounding of hooves behind him.

He turned to see a black-clad man on a piebald horse racing out of town. Alec hurried back in the direction he'd come from and found his mother lying on the ground, having been pushed to one side, and the door to the bank flung wide open. He crouched down beside his mother. She had a nasty cut over her eye and seemed a little dazed. "Oh, Mama, what happened?" he asked.

"That, that, that rapscallion robbed the bank," she exclaimed. "He pulled out his gun on poor Mr. Gately and pushed all of us aside. He was a brute. A brute."

"Are you hurt anywhere else?" he asked, lifting her hair a little so he could look at the cut more closely. She was as pale as milk and shaking like a leaf. Alec had never seen her so scared, so meek. He kissed her cheek.

"My ankle hurts, my wrist, and my back."

"Can you stand?"

"I don't know," she admitted cautiously. Alec helped her slowly to her feet, but she winced and hissed loudly at the pain when she put weight onto her right ankle. Alec lifted her up and carried her home, where he lay her tenderly upon her bed.

"I'm going to fetch the doctor," he said firmly. "You are not to move until I come back."

"Dr. Lancelot," she insisted, even now determined to get her own way.

"You'll get whoever is available," he said just as firmly. She didn't argue with him.

Alec ran across the road to the doctor's office. Nelly Graham, Dr. Lancelot's long-suffering nurse and secretary, greeted him with a grim smile. There were two other people in her waiting room, both with cuts and bruises. "They're from the bank robbery," she said. "I can't believe such a thing happened here in Iron Creek."

"My mother was hurt, too," Alec said. "I think it's probably just a bad sprain, but she's hurt her ankle, her wrist, and her back. I took her home, but I think she should see a doctor."

"Dr. Lancelot has been run off his feet today, but Dr. Anna just stopped by. She's finished for the day, but you might be able to catch her if you hurry. She said she was going down to the creek with Wilfred."

"I saw her just before it happened. I'll see if I can find her."

Alec hurried down toward the creek. He was pretty sure he knew where he might find Anna. She loved a spot where the creek swelled out a little and grew deeper, a little way downstream. A family of otters often played and hunted there, their sleek bodies darting through the waters. He strode quickly but carefully as he made his way along the slippery bank. There had been a lot of rain recently, and the late spring snows had left the ground sodden when they'd finally melted away just a week or so ago. It made the walk more than a little treacherous underfoot, and though not deep, Alec did not have any intention of ending up in the creek.

Alec heard Wilfred before he saw Anna. The little dog had obviously smelled him coming and came bounding toward him, jumping up at him and yelping excitedly. "Hey, fella," Alec said, bending down to him and playing with him a little.

Anna emerged from behind a large oak tree. "Alec, what are you doing here?"

"Looking for you," he said. "There was a robbery at the bank. Several people got hurt, including Mama. Dr. Lancelot is busy, so I wondered if you might come and check her over?"

Anna had a look of concern on her face. "You think your mother will let me treat her?"

"Honestly?" He shrugged. "No, I don't. But I don't intend to give her a choice. She can't bear weight on her ankle, she's hurt her wrist, and she has a nasty cut over her eye I think may need stitching. She needs help, and I'll make sure she accepts it."

"Then we'd best hurry," Anna said. "Can you carry Wilfred? I don't want him running off again, given we need to get somewhere in a hurry."

She picked up her skirts as Alec picked up the dog, and the two of them made their way back to Alec's home. He shut Wilfred in the yard, then showed Anna up to his mother's room. Mama scowled when she saw her. "Be polite, Mama,"

Alec warned her. "She's here to help. And, no, Dr. Lancelot could not come instead. The man is busy."

While he was talking, Anna moved to the washstand by his mother's bed and washed her hands thoroughly. She dried them on the cloth hanging below the basin, then turned to the bed and opened her medical bag. Alec hadn't even realized that she had been carrying it; he'd grown so used to seeing her with it since she'd moved to Iron Creek.

"Mr. Jenks told me that you hurt your wrist and your ankle, Mrs. Jenks," she said in a calm and patient voice. "But, if you don't mind, I'd like to look at the wound on your head first?"

Mama nodded. "My back is very sore, too," she admitted in a quiet voice.

"We'll look at that, too, then."

Anna turned to Alec. "Could you fetch me some clean cotton cloths and some hot water in perhaps two, maybe three bowls?" she asked him. He nodded and hurried downstairs.

When he returned, Anna had finished her initial assessment. She looked serious but not overly concerned. Alec placed the tray on Mama's bedside cabinet and watched her carefully clean the tools that she'd taken from her bag in the hot water, then hold them in a flaming taper from the fireplace. She made Mama lie flat, then gently and tenderly began to clean the wound on her head. Mama whimpered a little but did not complain, not even when Anna began to tie the stitches.

After a final clean with some iodine, Anna stood back to admire her work. The stitches were neat and tiny, much more so than the ones Alec recalled Dr. Lancelot giving him when he'd cut open his arm a few years ago. "Now, may I look at your back?" she asked Mama. "Could you roll over for me?" She turned to Alec again, obviously wanting to get him out of the room. "And could you go and fetch me some hot, sweet tea? It's good for calming the nerves."

Alec didn't need to be asked twice. He went downstairs and puttered around making the tea. He listened to the conversation upstairs and was surprised at how civil it was. Anna seemed to be working her magic. He'd hoped that the two women would eventually find some common ground if he could get them in a room together, but things seemed to be going much better than he'd expected. Perhaps it was because his mother needed Anna's knowledge and skills. Perhaps she was still a little out of sorts due to the robbery. Whatever it was, it gave Alec hope.

CHAPTER 13

May 1880, Iron Creek, Minnesota

Anna checked in on Mrs. Jenks every couple of days. The older woman never looked exactly pleased to see her, but she was always polite enough. After a few visits, it was time to remove the bandage above Mrs. Jenks' eye and take out the stitches if all was well. "The wound above your eye is healing very nicely," Anna said as she looked it over. She pulled a few items from her bag and set them on the table. "Might I perhaps have some hot water and clean cloths?"

"There's some by the stove," Mrs. Jenks said, pointing to the kettle and pile of clean white cotton rags.

"Thank you," Anna said. She fetched them and poured some of the water into a bowl, then carefully removed the stitches and handed Mrs. Jenks a mirror to look at the tiny scar that was left. "In a month or two, the scar will be barely visible to anyone but those right up close."

"You did an excellent job," Mrs. Jenks said a little grudgingly as she looked at the well-healed wound on her forehead. "Very neatly done." Anna smiled and tried to focus on the words rather than the woman's tone as she checked over Mrs. Jenks wrist, ankle, and back. She could see no permanent damage to any of them and told her patient so.

Mrs. Jenks nodded, stood up, reached for the cane she'd hooked over the tabletop, and walked a little unsteadily toward the stove, where she put a kettle of water on to boil. Anna took the opportunity to observe how much better her movement was now the swelling from the sprain had subsided, but she still thought that Mrs. Jenks should be recovering faster than she was. She suspected that while Alec still showed no signs of moving back into his own house, daily visits from her son were perhaps behind the older woman's desire to play upon her wounds a little longer.

"And you seem to be getting around a little easier now," she said innocently. "Perhaps you could try walking outside a little more. The weather is much improved, and the fresh air and sunshine would do you good."

"Thank you for suggesting that Alec make me a cane. It has been a great help." The older woman ran her finger over the carefully molded iron handle, pointedly ignoring Anna's suggestion.

"Might I have a look?" Anna asked. "I have never seen a cane with an otter's head for a handle before."

"My Alec knows how I love them," Mrs. Jenks said, unwittingly letting her guard down for just a moment.

"I do, too," Anna said as Mrs. Jenks sat back down and handed her the cane. Alec was definitely an artist. He had created a truly lifelike image of the sweet water creature, with its curious eyes and alert posture. "He is so clever with metal."

"Yes, he is." Mrs. Jenks looked sad for a moment. "We, his father and I, wanted him to become a doctor—or at least a lawyer. He was so clever, and the studying would have been no trouble for him at all. But no. He wanted to be a blacksmith." She shook her head, remembering the moment when the young Alec had approached them with the news.

"I think my parents were just as concerned for me when I told them I wished to be a doctor," Anna said softly. "They wanted the best for me and, to them, that meant staying safe and sticking to what was expected."

"That's exactly it," Mrs. Jenks exclaimed. "We wanted him to live comfortably, to have more than we did, to be respected in the community." She paused for a moment. "But he found a way to achieve all of that without us, without becoming a doctor."

"You have every right to be proud of him," Anna said. Then instantly regretted it when the older woman frowned.

"Who are you to tell me whether or not to be proud of my son?" she demanded.

"I didn't say that," Anna protested. "I was just—"

"I don't care what you were 'just'," Mrs. Jenks cut in. "You have not earned the right to tell me anything about how to raise my son or whether I've done a good enough job of it."

Taken aback by Mrs. Jenks' unprompted outburst, Anna made her excuses and left the house. She was still trying to make sense of what had changed and why it had happened so very suddenly when Sheriff Hanson stepped out of his office. He saw her and waved for her to join him. He was a handsome man, lean and rangy, with aquiline features and a day-old shadow of a beard on his chiseled chin. He always wore all black, with a black and silver holster at his hips, which carried two shining pistols—one on each side. She'd seen him draw those pistols only once, and he was as fast as the bullets he shot from them. If she were a criminal, she would not want to be chased by the likes of Matt Hanson, that was for sure.

She crossed the street and stepped up onto the porch. "Good day, Sheriff," she said. "How can I help you?"

"Got a fool in the cell, drank too much. Let his mouth run a little too much in the saloon last night. I think it's just cuts and bruises, but could you look him over? Check it's no more than that?"

"I'd be delighted," she said, following him inside. "Have you heard any more about the man that robbed the bank? Are there any clues?"

"Not a word," he said, shaking his head. They went through the empty office and out back to the cells. "But we've got a good likeness of him drawn now. All those who saw him say it looks just like him. We'll catch him."

"I hope you do."

The smell hit her as soon as Sheriff Hanson opened the door to the long stone corridor to the cells. The mixture of stale alcohol, smoke, sweat, vomit, and urine was no worse than the stench of some of the tenements and so-called hospitals that she'd worked at back in Boston, though. There were three large cells, all made of solid iron bars, forged and installed by Alec. Anna didn't doubt that they could hold even the strongest or most dastardly criminals. The sheriff gave her an apologetic look as he took a ring of keys from a hook by the door and walked along the corridor to a cell at the very end. He let her inside the cell, where a man was lying on the floor, barely moving.

"How long has he been lying there like that?" she asked.

"All night since I brought him in."

"He's not woken at all?"

"No, and I know that's unusual. It's why I'm glad you were walking by so early."

Anna rolled the man onto his back. He was burning up with fever, his breathing was slow and labored, and his pulse was weak. She checked his throat and his stomach and looked inside his mouth. His breath was even worse than the stench of the cell block. She lifted his lids to look at his eyes, then listened carefully to his chest. "I think this man needs a hospital bed more than he needs a jail cell floor. I think he has pneumonia."

"He's not committed a crime, other than being a bit of an idiot," Sheriff Hanson said.

"The fever quite probably made him delirious. That can happen sometimes, and people can say things they'd never normally say," Anna explained.

"He's free to go, but I don't know where to take him. Nearest hospital is in Grand Marais, and he doesn't look well enough to make that trip to me."

"You're right. He isn't. I'll ask around and see if there's anyone who can take him in and nurse him for a few days."

Anna's first port of call was Nelly. The kindly old nurse gave her a pallid smile and pointed to the two beds that Dr. Lancelot kept for patients who needed twenty-four-hour care. "We've got no room here, so I can't take him."

"What do you do when there's no room here at the clinic?" Anna asked.

"We have a couple of volunteers in the town who will take a patient in if they don't need more specialist care," Nelly said. "But otherwise, families look after each other."

"So, who are those volunteers?"

"Well, the minister at the church often takes people in, but he's visiting family. You could try Mrs. Jenks, but you'd know better than I would if she's ready for that."

Anna really didn't want to have to go back to the Jenks' house, but it was looking like she had no choice. The man in the sheriff's cell needed care, and she did not have the space in her tiny cottage or the time to care for him as there seemed to be an unprecedented amount of sick people around town for the time of year. It seemed there was no other option available, and Mrs. Jenks was well enough. Anna was sure that she was playing on her injuries, as little as they were, for attention from her son.

Reluctantly, she made her way back to the Jenks' house and knocked on the door. Anna could hear Mrs. Jenks' shuffling footsteps and the clank of her cane as she drew closer. Then the door opened. "What do you want?" the older woman demanded, her expression sour.

"I need to ask a favor," Anna said, trying her best to ignore the woman's unpleasant demeanor. "I have a man with pneumonia in need of care. He's not a local man, so I don't know much about him, but Nelly said that you are the person to turn to when someone is in trouble. I'd be personally very grateful if you might take him in for a few days until his fever breaks."

"I'm not well enough," Mrs. Jenks grumbled and went to shut the door in Anna's face.

"I think you are," Anna said. "And I also think that having someone to care for will help your ankle and wrist to regain their strength."

"I will not take anyone into my house while Alec is not here. It wouldn't be right. You said yourself; he's from out of town. We don't know a thing about him. He could be a bandit or a killer. I will not risk my life for the likes of that."

Anna sighed. "If I perhaps spoke with Mr. Jenks and asked him to come home, might you consider it then?" she asked wearily.

Mrs. Jenks' eyes lit up momentarily; then, she scowled again. "I won't have you interfering in matters between my son and me, either. You have no right to meddle, whatever sway you might think you have."

Anna had tolerated enough of her nonsense. "Mrs. Jenks, if I hold any sway over Mr. Jenks at all, it is because I listen to him and want what is best for him. Whether you like it or not, he and I are good friends. If truth be told, I love him. I wish with all my heart things had not come to where they are now. I want you to like me, to approve of me, and to realize that I have no desire to come between you and your son. I do not even wish to come between you and the care you take of him because I know how much that matters to you. But you cannot see that because you choose to close your eyes to me. And to what might make him content." She paused for a moment. Mrs. Jenks looked stunned. "I love your son and have from the very first. We would already be wed if it weren't for you and your nonsense. But you had already let him have his one rebellion. That was quite enough, wasn't it? Heaven forbid he might want to choose more than his own profession!" She turned and walked down the path and back onto the street. "If you do not care for this man, he might die. Whatever you think of me, as a good Christian woman can you truly bear to have that upon your conscience?"

Anna walked back to the sheriff's office. Sheriff Hanson had moved the man from the cells into his office, where he'd set up a trundle bed. He'd placed a cold compress upon his sweat-covered brow and piled blankets upon him to try to stop his shivering. "How is he?" Anna asked.

"As well as can be expected," Sheriff Hanson said with a shrug. "I've done all I can. Is there anywhere he can go where he'll be more comfortable?"

"For the moment, no. But I'm working on it," Anna said. "Just give me a few more hours."

She stopped off at the forge but didn't go in when she saw Mrs. Jenks was there. The older woman was almost puce with rage and yelling at her son, but Anna couldn't make out what she was saying. With a heavy sigh, she went home, where she was greeted by the ever-effusive Wilfred, who smothered her hands and face with licks as she bent down to hug him tightly. "What would I do without you on a bad day?" she asked him.

She looked around the tiny cottage that Dr. Lancelot and Alec had arranged for her use and wondered if it was possible for her to bring the man here. She was not really at home enough for it to be viable, and he would need someone with him at all times, at least for the next couple of days. But if it was the only option, then that was what she would have to do. Anna could sleep in her chair down here by the fire while he slept in her room upstairs.

She fixed herself a simple lunch of bread and cheese and ate it, looking out of the window. As she finished the last bite, she was surprised to see Alec bounding up onto her porch and banging on the door. She must have been deeply lost in her thoughts as she'd not even seen him coming. Anna hurried to open the door and was about to apologize to him for the way she'd spoken to his mother when he reached out and placed a gentle finger over her lips. "Don't," he said. "She told me everything, and I must say, you are braver than I." He smiled at her.

"It just came out," Anna admitted. "I truly didn't mean it to. I've been biting my tongue for weeks."

"I know, she has that effect. But she'll take your patient, and I will move back in. Until he leaves, at least."

"You'd do that?"

"I would for you. Don't you know that you only ever need to ask?"

CHAPTER 14

June 1880, Iron Creek, Minnesota

Alec watched as the two women he loved most in the world circled each other. Each was as wary as a cat, neither ever really trusting the words of the other at face value, though they seemed to have come to some manner of truce during the weeks of the stranger's recovery. Anna called by often, with laudanum and tonics to ease the man's pain and try to stimulate his system back to health. His mother took them and followed Anna's instructions to the letter. A grudging professional respect, if nothing else, seemed to be growing between them. And they were rewarded with the man's recovery—and the knowledge of his name: Nathaniel Holden.

But there was still a heavy undercurrent of dislike there, too, at least on his mother's side. Anna seemed to have accepted that she would never be liked by Mama, but Alec had not. He could see no good reason for it other than jealousy, and his mother should know that there was nobody who could ever take her place in his life. Just because he cared for Anna did not mean that he loved his mother any less. Yet, he did not know how he would ever convince Mama of that simple fact.

The early summer days were bright and full of promise, and Alec and Anna spent more time together as the days lengthened. Alec never ceased to be amazed by her strength and ability to shrug off the negativity of others. Her demeanor was almost always sunny, and everyone in town spoke of her in glowing terms. He did not understand why his mother could not see the woman that everyone else did.

"She won't let herself see it," Dr. Lancelot said to Alec when he came in to have his horse reshod. "She's had you all to herself your whole life. It's not easy for a woman like your mother to step back."

"You make it sound as though she isn't rational and sensible," Alec said.

"In this, perhaps she is not. However, I would have vouched for her ability to see through the nonsense to the very heart of any other matter. I've always had the utmost respect for your dear mother and your dear, departed Papa, too. He was a good friend to me over the years.

"He always spoke highly of you and was grateful to you for the position in Grand Marais."

"I did nothing but send a short letter about my brilliant

college friend," Dr. Lancelot said with a wistful smile. "I think more and more often of the times we shared back at medical school, how full of hope and excitement we were. It's why I like Dr. Anna. She is full of optimism for the future—for what she can achieve for the betterment of everyone. And she'll do it, too, if she's not burdened with becoming a wife and mother."

"It isn't right, is it," Alec said thoughtfully as he picked the horse's hooves clean before fitting the new shoes. "It's not right that women like Dr. Anna should be expected to give up everything when they are wed."

"No, it is not. No man of our acquaintance would tolerate it. And if a widower is left alone to care for his children, nobody complains if he hires a nanny and continues to work. But woe betide a wife or a widow who wishes to do the same."

"Do you think things will ever change?"

"Perhaps," the elderly doctor said with a sad smile. "But it won't be in my lifetime. Nor perhaps yours, my boy."

They did not speak while Alec fitted the shoes carefully to each hoof. Alec couldn't help wondering how old Dr. Lancelot was. He knew he'd been one of his father's contemporaries but recalled his father saying that Dr. Lancelot had come to medicine late, after following a successful career elsewhere. Papa had not known what that had entailed, and it seemed that nobody had ever asked.

Dr. Lancelot paid him and walked his horse to the gates.

"I'm glad you brought her to us," he said. "The town needs her. I need her. If I am ever to retire, I need to know you are all in good hands—and hers are some of the best I've ever seen."

"Are you warning me away from her, Dr. Lancelot?"

"Not at all. I think it is probably far too late for that for both of you. Though I know, she misses her family terribly, and at times wishes she had not left them behind."

"She has barely mentioned them to me," Alec mused. "I wonder why?"

"Perhaps because talking of them only makes her miss them more."

"Do you think she might leave?"

"I don't know. She is a complex woman. So independent in so many ways, yet there are claims on her heart. Her family, her work."

"So, you are warning me that I may not be enough for her?"

"No, my boy. I am simply making sure you know that she is already married. To medicine. And she has a family that she loves. You will always have to compete, perhaps with both of those."

"As a wife so often does with a husband's family and career," Alec mused thoughtfully.

"Exactly," Dr. Lancelot said, wagging his finger excitedly. "Can you be a wife to her? Because that is what she will need. There are many pressures to being a physician, and a good wife can help with many of them."

"So, why have you never married?" Alec asked, knowing the question was perhaps too personal.

"Because the woman I loved fell in love with one of my dearest friends instead of me. And because I was blessed to find dear Nelly very early on in my career." He grinned, but his implication was clear enough to Alec.

"You were in love with Mama?"

A dreamy look passed over the old man's face. "Oh, yes, indeed I was. We met through our fathers when I was no more than eighteen. She was about thirteen or fourteen then, but she was so smart. She put all of us boys to shame with her quick wit and wry humor. She wrote to me while I served in the army and even came to a ball at the medical school with me, just as friends, of course. It was there that she met your father, and I don't think she's seen me since."

This revelation played upon Alec's mind as the afternoon wore on. By the time he was heading back home for his supper, a plan had started to form. His mother was lonely. She needed someone to care for as she had his father and as she did him. She had been the perfect, supportive doctor's wife once. Why not again? Dr. Lancelot was a good, kind man, and Alec knew that his mother respected him greatly.

But how to do it?

He wondered if Anna would help him or think him a fool for meddling. But it seemed so clear to him that this could be the perfect solution. Dr. Lancelot clearly still loved Mama. They had much in common and shared many memories.

Mama lit up when he entered a room, whether it be mass or a dance, a town council meeting or a picnic down at the creek. He understood her, and she understood him.

There was only one flaw in his plan. His mother was still in love with his father. How could he convince her that she would not be disloyal to his father's memory if she chose to love again? There had to be a way. He needed Mama to be happy and settled in a life where she had purpose before he would be able to wed himself. He was sure of that. But it was going to be hard work.

"What are you plotting?" Anna asked him as she entered the yard at a quarter past six.

"I have an idea," he said, excited and nervous to tell her all at once.

"Do tell," she encouraged him.

"Well, it will sound silly, but Dr. Lancelot was here earlier, so I could shoe his horse. And he, well…" he trailed off and looked her deep in the eyes. "You must promise not to tell a soul."

"I promise," she said solemnly.

"Well, it would appear that he has been in love with Mama for over forty years."

"Goodness," Anna said, shaking her head. "That is a long time to not be noticed by someone."

"I know, but do you think we can get her to notice him?"

Her brow furrowed, and she looked perplexed. "Whatever do you mean?"

"I mean that I think Mama needs a new husband. Who better than the man who has loved her for all of his adult life?"

Anna looked at him as though he was quite mad. "Your mother will never marry anyone as long as she thinks you need her."

"We cannot marry until she has someone else to look after," Alec pointed out. "Can't you see? Her biggest fear is not losing me. She knows that she never will. No wife takes the place of a mother or vice versa. Such a thing would be quite terrible. She knows I love her and knows I need her, though not as much as I did as a boy. No, my mother is the wife of a doctor. Don't you see that with my father's passing, her career disappeared overnight? Everything she had done for him became nothing."

"You think your mother's vocation was to be a doctor's wife?" Anna said slowly as if she was still trying to get such a thing to make sense in her mind. "You may have a point. I know my own mother might well agree that wives have to become skilled in many ways they never imagined when they marry a farmer, for example. I never thought of it that way for doctors or lawyers. But it could be true. After all, many doctors' wives are nurses and often run their practices as well as running the home and raising the children."

"That is why my mother is always in such a good mood when she has someone sick to care for. She is never happier, in fact. With my Aunt Lilah, with Mr. Holden, with my father.

Even the Jellicoe twins, who always seem to have some ailment or another."

"And it may also be why she is always so angry with me. I do not need a husband in order to follow my vocation," Anna said perceptively. Alec hadn't considered that, but it was certainly as good an explanation for his mother's hostility as anything else might be. "She was brought up in a time when a woman's only role was to be a wife. And she picked the kind of wife she wanted to be."

"I wonder if that was why poor Dr. Lancelot didn't win her hand before she met my father. He was in the army, and she hadn't chosen to be the wife of a soldier," Alec mused.

"But he was at medical school with your father, wasn't he?" Anna queried.

"Yes, he was. But perhaps Mama thought he might be fickle and change his mind about what he wanted to do again. Perhaps she thought he was studying medicine just to please her."

"And she wanted to know whoever she chose wasn't going to change his mind."

It was far-fetched, but it was the sort of thing he could imagine his mother doing. She had always been so methodical and so prepared for every eventuality. She made the most troubling times seem straightforward, as if she had a plan for everything that could possibly go wrong. At least it felt that way at times. But she hadn't planned for Papa passing away when he had. She had been lost and rudderless. She had lost her position as a physician's wife overnight. It must have felt like such a cruel blow.

The more Alec considered it, the more it made sense. And if Andrew Lancelot hadn't proved that he was committed to the practice of medicine, then no man had. He just had to get Mama to see him as she perhaps had when she was a girl. She had obviously cared for him if she had written to him for all those years. They had obviously been close. He just had to remind her of that, somehow.

After he and Anna had finished their evening walk, he went home for his supper. Mr. Holden was already sitting at the table when he arrived. "Good evening, Mr. Jenks," he said politely.

"Good evening, and how are you feeling today?"

"Much better, thanks to you and your dear Mama. I cannot thank you both enough for taking in a stranger and caring for me as you have."

"Mama has always had a way with invalids," Alec said with a smile as his mother entered the room.

"It is what is expected of you when you marry a doctor," she said piously, and at that moment, Alec knew he was right.

"I shall just go and wash and change," he said. He kissed her cheek and smiled to himself.

"You do that. I left a letter on the mantel in your room. It arrived this afternoon on the stagecoach, addressed to us both. It is from some of your father's colleagues. They wish to hold a memorial dinner for him," she said. There was a glimmer of pride in her eyes. "I don't know if it is right that we should attend. It is, perhaps, a little morbid after all this time, but I should so hate to let your father down."

"I'll look at it," Alec said. He grinned as he made his way along the corridor and up the stairs. It seemed that providence had sent him the perfect way to throw his mother and Dr. Lancelot together—and all while honoring his father. Alec wasn't the kind of man to believe in fate or destiny; he believed a man made his own luck, but he couldn't help thinking that this was perhaps a sign that his father approved of his plan.

CHAPTER 15

June 1880, Iron Creek, Minnesota

"Would you please come with me tomorrow?" Alec asked Anna as they took one of their evening walks. "I know that things are not as they should be between you and my mother, but I really want you to be there."

"I am honored," Anna said, "but I do feel that it is an event for family and those who knew your father, and I am neither."

Alec gave her a sad smile. "You would be family if it weren't for my mother. You do know that I want you to be my wife and would have made you such long ago were it not for her stubborn nature, don't you?"

Anna sighed. She did know that. And until recently, it had not mattered that he continued to put his mother's feelings before her own. She was coming to wonder if it was all just an excuse, that Alec might always find a reason not to make their friendship something more permanent. Alec did not seem to be the kind of man to willingly deceive, though, and she was sure that his feelings for her were real enough, but he had never told her he loved her, only that he cared for her. How was she to know if she was waiting for something that may never come?

He took her hands, and a sensation of excitement flooded through her, as always happened whenever he touched her, even in the lightest and most innocent of ways. She looked into his eyes and willed him to dip his handsome head further to steal a kiss. But he never did. He was always the perfect gentleman. "You know, I have an idea, Anna. Though you may think it silly, I think this dinner in honor of my father may serve as just the prompt we need," he said earnestly.

Anna shook her head. "I do not think that your mother will consider another husband. She is not the type to remarry, no matter what her past feelings for Dr. Lancelot might have been."

"I had always thought the same thing, but I have changed my mind," Alec said excitedly. "She is bored and lonely. She misses not just my father but the lifestyle being his wife provided. I filled that void for a time, but my needs are not sufficient. And challenging though they are, the Jellicoe twins do not make up for it either. She needs to be needed. Dr. Lancelot has loved her for more than forty years, and he is a doctor who needs a wife capable of supporting him."

"I do understand your logic, but it's not that. You forget about feelings. Your mother loved your father deeply for fitting her requirements, as you put it. But Dr. Lancelot has Nelly, who has been his right hand in the way a wife might have been. He has proven that a wife is not a necessity. What makes you think that he might wish to take a wife after all these years as a bachelor?"

"Love. Love is what makes me think he wants a wife. And we have two doctors in town now. Nelly is already stretched a little thinly between you both, and you will not be taking a wife to assist you."

"I would not be permitted to do such a thing," Anna said, laughing at his clearly thought-through arguments. "You are right, of course. We have already had to call upon your mother for assistance, and that need for help will only increase as the town grows. And should I marry, I doubt my husband would be willing to give up his own profession to support me in mine."

"So, please come with me. Help me to bring them together. I truly think it is for the best."

He looked so keen, so eager, so like a puppy that just wanted to be loved, Anna could not resist his plea. "I will help," she said. "And I will attend. But if this all goes wrong, it's on your own head, Alec Jenks. I will take no part in your scheming further than this one night. Your mother hates me enough as it is; I will not incur her further wrath by pushing her into something if I see no sign of her wishing such a thing to occur."

"I cannot ask for more than that," Alec said, beaming. He bent his head and pressed a chaste kiss upon her cheek, then moved to pull away, but by no more than a few inches. Anna felt her breath catch. She waited, not daring to move. Would this be the moment that he finally claimed her lips as his own? She would not resist, though she knew that such behavior would be highly inappropriate, and they would be the talk of the town given they were standing right outside the general store where anyone might see them.

Alec hesitated. Anna could feel his warm breath upon her cheek. She tilted her head slightly, so he might kiss her more easily and closed her eyes. It felt like an eternity passed before he finally dipped his head and pressed his lips to hers. Anna's body went limp as his arms snaked around her waist, and he pulled her close against his warm, muscular body. Every cell in her body buzzed with life. But the kiss was over before it had even begun. Alec stepped away, clearing his throat a little and smoothing his vest, his face full of contrition.

"I am sorry," he said. "I should not have let myself get carried away like that."

Anna grinned at him. "I did not mind. In fact, I wouldn't mind it if you got carried away in such a manner more often."

"You are quite brazen," Alec said teasingly. He took her hand, and the two of them continued walking. "Is that why I love you?"

Anna stopped walking. "I'm sorry, what was that?" she said, stunned that he had finally said the three words that she had so longed to hear from him.

"I asked if your brazen nature was why I love you?" he said, a grin on his face as he watched her stunned reaction.

"You love me?" she queried again.

"For a doctor, you have terrible comprehension sometimes," he teased. "I love you. Is that easier to understand?"

"You love me," she echoed, feeling as though Christmas had come early. She had hoped but had not dared to let herself believe such a thing might be true. But there were still so many obstacles between them.

"I love you," he repeated. "And I would like to hope that you, perhaps, might feel the same way about me?"

His prompt made Anna laugh. "Now you are just fishing for my affections," she teased him back. "Would it mean as much if I just said it now, or would you rather I tell you when I truly mean it?"

"I would hope that you would truly mean it even if you told me now," Alec countered.

"I love you," she said simply. "I have from your very first letter. You were honest and good. You knew who you were and what you wanted, and it didn't matter to you if that was something different from what was expected. I couldn't help admire that. And probably rather importantly, you seemed quite content with the idea that I was a doctor and that my work might mean I would never be a wife in the way most men might expect."

"It was the same for me," he admitted. "You were so direct. I knew there would be no games, no silly nonsense about whether we did or did not suit each other, no endlessly behaving as society might expect. You were your own person. You had an interest and passion as great as my own, and I knew I need not ever fear that you would begrudge the time I have to spend at my work."

"You at least get to bed at a reasonable hour every night," Anna said, flattered by his words. They weren't the kind of compliment that many women would wish for, but they were everything Anna wanted to hear. From the first time they met, it had been uncanny how well they understood each other.

"I do, and I do not envy you the midnight emergencies and all-night vigils you have to bear."

They had reached her door. Anna reached up on tiptoe and kissed his lips, claiming them forever as her own. "Goodnight," she said to him softly as he embraced her.

"Goodnight," he whispered in her ear. "I do so hope you get some rest tonight."

Anna did. She woke with the dawn, feeling happy and refreshed. She fairly bounced through her morning and finished her house calls by midday, then went home where she bathed and dressed with particular care in order to attend the memorial dinner in Grand Marais with Alec and his mother.

When she saw a fine carriage pull up outside the Jenks'

house, she picked up her handbag and left the house. Alec had come outside and was checking over every inch of the carriage and the horses, clad in his fine evening wear. She reached him as he was picking up one of the animals' hind hooves to inspect its shoes. "Are you always so thorough?" she teased him.

"I am when the safety of those I love is at stake," he said. He put down the horse's hoof and smiled warmly at her. Anna felt a little awkward but decided to give him a little twirl as he seemed to want to look her over so carefully. "You look lovely," he said.

"Thank you."

Dr. Lancelot approached them. He looked very dapper in a finely tailored black evening suit and top hat, with a silver-topped cane in his hand. "Well, don't we make a fine party," he said as Mrs. Jenks appeared on the porch. Mama was wearing a ruby red silk gown and matching lace shawl, and her hair was pinned carefully in an extravagant knot. The entire effect made her appear ten years younger. She smiled when she saw her son and Dr. Lancelot, which took off another five. Anna had never seen her smile that way, with so much joy in her eyes.

Dr. Lancelot walked up the path to the porch and offered her his arm. Mrs. Jenks pulled the shawl more tightly over her shoulders and slipped her arm through his. They shared a look, the kind of look those who have known each other for a lifetime often do, and suddenly, Alec's crazy plan to push them together did not seem so far-fetched after all. Alec glanced at her, his eyes wide with hope. Anna nodded to him, letting him know without words that she saw the same thing that he was. There was definitely a spark between them, an attraction that Anna had not noticed before. Perhaps they hadn't either, at least not in a very long time. But the air crackled around them now.

Dr. Lancelot escorted Mrs. Jenks to the carriage and helped her inside, then jumped in behind her. Alec had just offered Anna his hand when Garrett Harding came racing along Main Street, dust billowing behind him and his horse. He drew the animal to a halt right by the carriage and leaped down from its back. Only then did Anna notice that the animal had no saddle. Garrett's eyes were wild with fear. "It's Katy," he said breathlessly. "She's vomiting and can't seem to stop."

Dr. Lancelot leaped out of the carriage. "I'll fetch my horse," he said.

Anna reached out a hand and placed it on his arm. "No, you go with Mrs. Jenks and Alec," she said calmly. "He was your friend. You belong at his memorial more than I do. I will stay and go to Mrs. Harding."

Dr. Lancelot nodded. His faith in her was something she cherished greatly. "You'll leave me a note to let me know how she does so I know when I get back?"

"I shall," she assured him. "Now, go, or you'll all be late."

The doctor got back into the carriage, where Anna could see him patting Mrs. Jenks' hand as he reassured her that there was nothing to worry about, that Anna would make sure Mrs. Harding was well. Alec started to get into the coach, then stopped. He closed the door. "I'll take Dr. Macdonald up the mountain. She may need assistance, and I can make sure she gets home safely in the dark."

"But your father?" Mrs. Jenks said plaintively.

"Would have attended a patient in need rather than a dinner in his own honor, and you know it," Alec said to her. He leaned in and kissed his mother's cheek. "Now, go. You and Dr. Lancelot will enjoy such an event far more than I. I never understand what all those doctors are talking about anyway." Mrs. Jenks nodded reluctantly, and Alec slapped the side of the carriage to tell the driver to go.

As it pulled away, Anna and Alec raced to the stables behind the doctors' office, where there were mounts always ready for such emergencies. Alec took Dr. Lancelot's bay stallion, and Anna took her own gray mare. They rode out onto Main Street, where Garrett Harding was anxiously waiting for them. "I can't lose her," he said, his emotions choking his voice so that it was barely recognizable.

"I will do all I can to ensure that doesn't happen," Anna said in a calm and firm voice before they all raced back up the mountain.

CHAPTER 16

June 1880, Iron Creek, Minnesota

Watching Anna work was fascinating. She was neat and methodical and gave clear directions. It made everyone around her, including Garrett, less afraid. When they'd arrived, poor Katy looked pale, thin, and exhausted. Within moments, Anna had sent the two men outside to wait on the porch while she examined her patient. When she let them back in, the air of panic in the house had been replaced by a calm professionalism that was as impressive as anything Alec had ever seen before.

When the two men returned, they found Anna cradling Katy. "When did this start?" she asked Katy as she swapped places with Garrett and began putting her instruments back into her black leather bag.

Katy started to speak but gagged. "It has been a few

weeks, I suppose," Garrett said, giving his wife a supportive look. "It didn't seem to be anything too much to be concerned about. But it has gotten worse and worse. She can barely keep water down, and even the smallest amounts of the simplest food just makes her retch and heave. She is exhausted, and then tonight, she just seemed to be unable to stop at all."

Anna gave him a sad smile. "I think that we have a peculiar situation here. From what Katy managed to tell me, from what you have told me, and from my observations, I think that Katy is with child again."

"She's...?" Garrett's eyes lit up briefly, but his expression of anxious fear returned as Katy began to retch once more. He held up the bucket by the side of the bed and stroked his wife's hair gently. "But this is surely something more than that?"

Anna gave him an understanding look. "Did she have any issues during her first pregnancy?"

"No," Katy croaked, wiping her lips and looking at Anna with an expression that said that Anna's conclusion was not such a revelation to her. "Jacob was no trouble at all, though I had a lot of false contractions in the final months."

"I think you have something we see very rarely. An extreme version of morning sickness," Anna said calmly. "In some mothers, we see it completely disappear by the fifth month of their pregnancy. In others, it can last the entire term. When was your last cycle, Katy?"

"I think two months ago," the poor woman said. "You

truly think I may have to survive another three months of this?"

"Possibly more," Anna said gravely. "I am sorry. I have only ever seen one other woman affected so badly since I began my training. It was hard on her, but I can assure you that she did make it through and gave birth to a very healthy, though small, set of twins." She smiled as she recalled them, and Alec could see that the story had given Katy and Garrett a brief moment of hope that all would turn out well in the end.

"The only thing I can do," Anna went on, "is stress that it is important that you keep trying to drink and eat as much as you can bear. You will need to keep your strength up. Even if all you can manage is a little broth or some dry bread, you must keep trying. I will come and check on you every day to make sure that you and the child are not in any danger, but you are going to need to rest and take care of yourself as much as you can. Is there anyone who can help you with Jacob?"

"I can ask my mother to come and stay with us," Garrett said.

Katy smiled at him. "That would be a wonderful idea," she said. "Why did we not think of that before? She's normally the first person we would turn to with something like this. She may have some tonic or other that might help."

Anna gave them a perplexed look. Alec grinned. "Garrett's mother is Ojibwe, a medicine woman," he explained. "She saved Katy's life once before."

"I don't know much about native medicine," Anna admitted, "but I certainly would never dismiss it out of hand as so many of my colleagues might. Perhaps I might learn a thing or two from her?"

"She'd be delighted," Garrett said, looking considerably more relieved than he had when he'd arrived outside Alec's door. "I'll ride over there now and fetch her if you wouldn't mind staying with my wife."

"We'd be glad to," Anna said, then paused as a thought crossed her mind. She turned to Alec. "Why don't you both go? I can get Katy cleaned up and put some freshly laundered sheets on the bed; then we can try to find some foods she might tolerate."

The two men nodded. Garrett kissed his wife, and then they headed out and mounted their horses. They rode in companionable silence for some miles before Garrett said anything. "She's quite extraordinary, isn't she?"

"She is," Alec agreed.

"And you met her because of an advertisement? Like I met Katy?"

Alec chuckled. He should have known that a wife would not be able to keep a secret from her husband. But he was not angry with Katy for telling Garrett. How could he be, especially under the circumstances? "I did."

"The wonders of the modern world never cease, do they?" Garrett said with a smile.

"No," Alec agreed. "I have to pinch myself most days to

make sure it is all real. She is everything I could ever have asked for and more."

"Katy, too," Garrett said softly, a haunted look of fear passing over his features once more. "I can't lose her."

"And you won't. Anna and your mother will take care of her. You know they will," Alec reassured his friend. "Both, in their own way, are so skilled and know so much. They'll keep her as safe as can be."

The two men spurred their horses to a gallop and raced toward the Ojibwe camp at Devil Track Lake. Spirals of smoke made their way upwards from the many birch bark lodges. Garrett urged his horse between them, nodding to friends and family as they made their way to Zaagasikwe's home at the very edge of the camp. He dismounted and knocked on the door. Aandeg, his grandfather answered his call. "My boy, it is good to see you, but I can tell by your eyes there is more to your visit than to please me."

Garrett indicated Alec should join them as they went inside. Zaaga was by the fire, making raspberry leaf tea. She gave her son a worried smile. "What is it, my son?"

"Katy is with child," Garrett said with a wan smile.

"This is good news," Aandeg said as he joined them at the fire, his old joints making it harder for him to move quickly these days.

"It is, but the doctor says that she has a very severe case of morning sickness."

Zaaga nodded. "Why did you not come to me before?" she asked.

"I didn't think," Garrett admitted. "And I think Katy kept the worst of it from me. She was so very bad tonight that I went to the nearest help I could think of. But we need you. Will you come and look after her and Jacob?"

"You need never ask," Zaaga said, giving her son an understanding look. "I will ride over tomorrow at first light."

She insisted that both men eat some of her excellent venison stew and drink some tea before she ushered them back out into the night. They rode back in silence. Alec couldn't help but think of the dangers that women faced—not just from bandits or accidents outside of the house, but from within. Having a child could be so very precarious, with so many things that might go wrong, and yet they still longed to be mothers. He'd seen his own mother's strength of will as he'd grown up. He had been an only child, but not because his parents hadn't wanted more. He knew that he was so special to his parents because they had been so unlucky before he came.

Now, however, was the first time that he'd been faced with the reality of what women went through to bring a healthy child into the world. There were dangers long before the birth, which itself could be life-threatening for both mother and child, and complications after the child came could risk a mother's life, too. Women truly were the stronger sex in both mind and body. To go through all they did and be so resilient was a wonder to him.

Katy was sleeping when they made it back to the Hardings' cabin, so Anna and Alec made their way back down the mountain. "You are quite amazing," Alec said as he helped Anna to dismount outside her little cottage. "The way you calm people who are so panicked. I could not do that."

"Then perhaps it is just as well that I became a doctor and you a blacksmith," she said with a weary smile.

"Indeed," Alec said, nodding.

They stood in the street, holding hands and looking into each other's eyes for a moment. "I wonder how your mother and Dr. Lancelot fared," Anna said, a mischievous look in her eye. "That was why you chose to come with me tonight, was it not? To give them time alone? You know full well that I am quite capable of getting myself to a patient no matter where they are or what time of day it might be."

"I do indeed, and you clearly know me too well," Alec said with a grin. "I saw the opportunity and thought there might never be a better one. I pray that they will realize what could be if they spend just a little time alone together."

"I still think you are overly optimistic, but I hope for our sake that you are right," Anna said. "But I am now very tired, so perhaps we might think about this more in the morning?"

Alec bent his head and kissed her tenderly, then reluctantly let her go. "I'll take the horses back to the stable," he said as she slowly moved away from him. "Good night."

"Good night," Anna said. She blew him a little kiss as she opened her door.

Alec took both animals' reins and watched until she had gone inside and lit a lamp. Then he walked slowly toward the doctors' stable, where he removed both horses' tack and brushed them down before saddling up the other two horses in their stalls in case they were needed. The work was simple and required little thought, and he found it soothing after the things he'd just witnessed. He would pray for Katy Harding, that she would be well again soon.

His mother was sitting at the kitchen table when he returned. "How is she?" she asked as she got up and began to make him some hot chocolate.

"Not well, but Zaaga will be moving in with them, and Dr. Macdonald will check on her every day," Alec explained.

"Is she with child?" Mama asked.

Alec didn't see any reason to deny it. His mother would not tell anyone else. "Yes."

"I was like that with you," she said, shaking her head. "I just couldn't stop. But I held on to the thought that at least you were still there, even if you were making me so sick. The others, I barely noticed anything until it was too late for them all."

She looked so sad as she remembered all the babies that might have been. Alec embraced her. "Thank you for going through all of that so I might be here today," he said softly.

"I'd do it all again," she said. "You were worth every bit of pain."

"I doubt that," he quipped, trying to lighten the mood.

"Perhaps that is the reason I've held onto you so tightly," Mama said softly as she poured the milk over the chocolate and whisked it lightly. "You were the only one that survived, my special child. I never wanted to let anything hurt you."

"And nothing ever has. Well, other than the odd burns when I don't pay enough attention to what I'm doing."

She smiled with him this time. "It is time to let you go, isn't it?"

"Mama, I will always be your son, whatever or whoever else comes into my life."

"I know that now."

They sat down at the table, with their hands cupped around their warm cups of cocoa. "You do? What changed your mind?"

"A rather long and sweet talk with dear Dr. Lancelot," Mama said with an enigmatic smile. "I remembered a lot of things I'd forgotten." She looked like a girl who'd just been to her first dance, mooning over the boy who had claimed her heart.

"Anything I should know more about?" Alec prompted gently.

"I don't know," she said. "Would you mind if there was?"

"Not one bit," he assured her. "I want you to be happy, and I can think of no finer man than Dr. Lancelot."

CHAPTER 17

July 1880, Iron Creek, Minnesota

It became quite a regular sight to see Dr. Lancelot crossing the road to escort Mrs. Jenks for a walk around midday and again at around half past six in the evening when he would join her and Alec for their evening meal. Anna found it rather sweet, this slow courtship after all their years of knowing each other. But still, Alec had not actually proposed to her or shown any intention of doing so. She did not wish to be presumptuous, but she was certain his feelings for her were as strong as her own were toward him, yet at this rate, Dr. Lancelot and Mrs. Jenks would be wed long before Alec even considered asking Anna for her hand.

But there were other matters to attend to, so she tried not to let it concern her too greatly. She was delighted to see that Katy Harding was faring much better under her mother-in-law's care. Her belly had finally started to grow, and both Zaaga and Katy were convinced that there was a strong possibility that she might be carrying twins. From their discussions about their experiences with such situations, Anna and Zaaga had concluded that those they knew who had suffered this way often had twins or triplets.

The two women had found much to talk about on Anna's daily visits up the mountain, and Anna was not above taking advice from the older woman. Her knowledge of plants, tonics, ailments, and diseases was in many ways superior to Anna's, thanks to her many years of treating her people. It was also a different kind of knowledge from that which Anna had been taught, and she was keen to learn all she could if it might help her patients in the future.

She worked hard and tried not to let her predicament concern her, but as each day passed with no proposal of marriage, she grew more convinced that there would never be one. Anna started to consider what would happen to her if that were the case. Could she bear to live in Iron Creek if Alec did not want her? Would she be able to watch him live his life without her in it? Or, even worse, with someone other than her in it? She loved him irrevocably, and if he asked her to, she would wait forever for him. But he didn't ask. He just continued to meet her to walk and talk, with nary a mention of their future or his intentions. Oh, he told her he loved her—often, in fact. He told her that he had never cared for anyone as he did for her. But he didn't ever say more about them being wed, even though his own mother was drawing closer to that outcome.

As July drew to an end, Anna was surprised to be invited to a party at the Jenks' house. She and Mrs. Jenks had been getting along better in recent weeks, but they were not what anyone might consider friends. Alec continued to make excuses for his mother's coldness toward her, but Anna was convinced that the older woman would never accept her as being good enough for her son.

She pinned her hair carefully and pulled on her best summer dress of floral cotton with a lace collar. Anna knew she looked pretty, and that knowledge gave her some semblance of confidence as she crossed the street to the Jenks' house. Everyone in town was in the large garden, where Mrs. Jenks' prized roses grew contentedly surrounded by a cornucopia of beautiful blooms of all sizes and colors. In the warm sunshine, the scent coming from them was intoxicating.

Mrs. Jenks looked radiant in a cream dress as she and Dr. Lancelot announced their engagement. Anna clapped along with everyone else, but though she was happy for them, their news brought her no closer to knowing what was in Alec's mind. For this party to have been arranged, he must have known about the older couple's intentions. If he had, then, surely, he should have asked her by now to be his wife?

But just as she was about to make her excuses and leave the party, wishing the happy couple all the luck in the world, Alec stepped up and started to tap a spoon against his glass.

"Ladies and gentlemen, I have another announcement I would like to make, if I may."

He glanced over at Anna. She felt a rush of heat from her belly all the way to the top of her head and was sure she must be blushing beet red. He wouldn't ask her there and then. In front of all these people. Would he? It felt so out of character, and Anna did not want to have to give an answer without time to think it all through. She had so many questions she needed to ask him, including the most important one: why had he waited so long to ask her?

Alec smiled at her and continued to speak. "Many of you have now met Dr. Anna. Some of you have been treated by her, and all of us here are glad to have been able to welcome her into our growing town. She has been a breath of fresh air. No matter what, she is always generous with her skills and knowledge and her time, and always has a kind word for everyone."

"Here, here," a few people in the crowd called out.

"Now, she's only been here a short while," Alec said, still grinning as though he was in possession of the greatest secret in the world. Anna cringed, fearful he truly did mean to ask her to marry him in public. She did not want that. He, of all people, should know her better than to put her on the spot in such a way.

But that was not what he said next. "I know that she misses her family terribly, so I am delighted to be able to welcome them here today, too."

Anna gasped, her hands involuntarily rising to cover her wide-open mouth as her mother and father appeared from inside the house. She ran up the steps onto the porch and wrapped her arms around them both. "Whatever are you doing here?" she asked between kissing them and receiving their kisses and embraces in return.

"We received a rather lovely letter from Mr. Jenks, there," her mother said, giving Alec a bashful look. Alec flushed a little. It was very endearing.

"He said that though you'd never tell us as much in your letters, and though you were happy as anything here in your work and all, you missed us and would like to see us again," her father explained.

"And he was right, though I'm not sure how he could know. I only ever spoke of missing you to Dr. Lancelot when I'd barely been here a month or two," Anna said. She narrowed her eyes at Alec and the good doctor, who had the decency to look a little guilty for conspiring behind her back.

"I told him," Dr. Lancelot admitted. "And I'd do it again to see the look of joy on your lovely face when you saw your parents again."

"Thank you," Anna said, moving to kiss him. Then, so it didn't look strange, she kissed Alec on his cheek, too.

This didn't make any sense to her. Why should he do such a kindly thing but not offer her the thing she wanted more than anything? He said he loved her. His every action supported his words, but he never said the words that mattered most.

But she was overjoyed to see her parents. They looked so happy and well. "Where are your things?" she asked, looking around meaninglessly as if they would have just left them on the porch. "We can go back to the cottage and get you settled in."

"We don't need to," her dad said, looking a little sheepish. "We've got a place to stay. Perhaps you'd like to come and see it?"

Anna gave him a puzzled look. "You have a place? But there's no hotel or boarding house in town."

"We know," her mom agreed. A grin on her face said she was bursting to tell Anna something and had been sworn to secrecy.

"What is it that you are keeping from me?" Anna asked.

"Come with us," her father said grinning like a boy. They took her hands, and the three of them went out onto Main Street and walked along it to the very end of town, where a grand, new house had been being built over the past month or two. The house was now finished.

"Welcome to Iron Creek's very first hotel," her father said proudly.

"But it's huge," Anna exclaimed.

"Yes, but not as large as the farm," her mother said with a smile. She led Anna up the steps and into a grand hallway. An oak staircase rose from the very center of the room, leading to a balustraded gallery with several doors leading off it. "What do you think?"

"I'm wondering what the two of you know about running a hotel and why you aren't at home on the farm. I'm wondering if this is all a crazy dream. I'm wondering what happened to your dream of buying that piece of land next to ours?"

Her parents laughed. "Well, we were about to purchase it when your mother hurt her leg. Nothing serious," her father explained quickly when Anna gave them an accusatory look for not telling her about such a thing. "It took her longer than usual to heal, and it's not been quite right since."

"Some of my chores were suddenly too much for me," her mother added. "And I was tired all the time. We sat down and discussed it and decided that taking on more work was probably not the best of ideas, so we put it off."

"We often talked about our time in Boston with you at Mrs. Phelps' house, and we thought about maybe selling up and buying a boarding house in the city. Things would be much easier for us, and all the things we need would be there," her father said.

"All of that makes perfect sense, but not this," Anna said, looking around and gesturing around the grandeur of the building they were standing in. "Mom, Dad, I just don't understand."

"Well, your Mr. Jenks wrote to us and told us how much you missed us, my darling," her mom said, putting an arm around Anna's waist. "And we wrote back and said to him how we'd maybe like to come and visit if that was the case.

We asked if there was a hotel or a boarding house where we might stay."

"And he said no," Anna said, suddenly seeing where they had gotten this crazy idea. "You were going to use the money you got, that windfall, to come and see me?"

They both nodded. Anna pulled them both close and hugged them tightly as she tried to hold back tears. She was so very glad to see them and so very amazed that they had kept something like this from her for so long. And Alec was to blame for this. He had conspired with them to keep this from her so she wouldn't try to talk them out of it. Their being in town would mean that Anna couldn't now leave even if she wanted to, even if Alec never proposed. How could she, when they had given up everything they had ever known?

"Yes, but then the gentleman who bought our grain came to us and asked if he might buy the farm outright, not just our produce," her dad explained. "It was too good an opportunity. Everything just fell into place. All your letters said what a wonderful town this was and how happy you were here, so we figured we would be, too."

Anna kissed his cheek and smiled. They had never done anything so spontaneous in their lives. They were the kind of people who struggled to change the supplier they used for anything, and the farmhouse had not been altered one iota in all of Anna's lifetime. Mom had patched and mended every piece of clothing they owned until there was more patch than garment. They hated to buy anything new, but now they had bought land and built a hotel hundreds of miles from their home to start a new life. It was quite the turnaround.

"Alec helped us to acquire the land here and has been overseeing the work to build this wonderful hotel, and now we are here to open it up."

Anna shook her head in disbelief. She could hardly believe what she was hearing, but she had never been so happy to see her family. She had a lot she wanted to discuss with Alec Jenks, but for the time being, she was just going to enjoy spending time with them, knowing that there would be no goodbye at the end of it. They would be staying in Iron Creek forever, and that made her so very happy.

CHAPTER 18

*A*ugust *1st 1880, Iron Creek, Minnesota*

The whole town was crammed into the back room of the saloon. Alec was still amazed that his God-fearing mother was prepared to be wed there, but in her mind it was the only church in town. He'd tried to convince her that the minister at the Presbyterian church would be happy to let Father Paul undertake the marriage ceremony there, but Mama would not hear of it.

As she wouldn't budge, he'd paid a fortune to have flowers brought in from the market at Grand Marais so they could fill the room with elegant blooms, along with the ribbons Judd had ordered for him that now dangled from the ceiling, hiding the more pedestrian meeting room underneath it all. Dr. Lancelot joined him and checked things over one last time.

"You've done a fine job," he said, slapping Alec on the back. "Thank you."

"It is my pleasure," Alec assured him. And it truly had been. Whatever it took to get his mother out of his house and married to the man who had loved her for years was worth it.

"You are sure you don't mind me marrying your mother? I know how close you and your father were, and I always had a huge amount of respect for him."

"I know that," Alec said. "And he knew that. And more importantly, Mama knows that. It is her choice. You are her choice. She always cared for you."

"But I missed my chance," Dr. Lancelot said with a smile. "If I'd only asked her when I'd intended to, she may never have even met your father."

"Then I am glad you did not because I am rather glad to have been born," Alec joked.

Dr. Lancelot smiled, but it was brief. "Don't wait too long," he warned Alec. "You may already have done so, you know?"

Alec frowned. He feared the same thing. Since the arrival of her parents in Iron Creek, he had barely seen Anna. At first, he'd given the family time to get reacquainted. They had been a long time apart and needed time and space. But after a while, he had realized that Anna was still rebuffing his calls to resume their walks together and spending all her time working. Of course, he'd had the wedding to arrange as his mother and Dr. Lancelot had not wished to waste any time. "At our age you must grab every chance when it arrives," Dr. Lancelot had said.

Between them they never seemed to have time for each other, and their conversations were stilted and awkward when they did meet. The easy familiarity they had once shared seemed to have disappeared. It was hard to bear. Alec feared that he had been a fool, that his determination to see his mother settled and out of his home had pushed their relationship past its limits. As he fingered the ring box in his pocket, he wondered if his grand plan to propose to Anna that evening was too little, too late.

But there was no time to think about that now. There was a wedding in his immediate future, even if that wedding was his mother's. It was his duty to give her hand to Dr. Lancelot, and he would not ruin her big day by dwelling on his fears. His mother deserved happiness, and he was sure she would find it with the kindly man standing to his side, his bright eyes full of joy that the woman he had loved for so long would finally be his bride.

"I will see you in less than an hour," Alec said. He took his leave and hurried home to bathe and dress.

When he entered the kitchen, his mother was having her hair done by a much healthier-looking Katy Harding and a smiling Mrs. Macdonald. Nelly was busy making everyone copious cups of tea. "You're here," his mother exclaimed. "There's no time, and you look like you've been out in the fields."

Alec looked down at his shirt and pants. He wasn't fit for a wedding, but he wasn't dirty or disheveled. "I shall be barely a moment," he promised her. He glanced at Mrs. Macdonald. "Will Anna be joining us here or at the church?"

"At the church, I believe," Mrs. Macdonald said. "She's helping her father check in some guests at the hotel. So many people from out of town this weekend, all here for your mother."

"I'm glad we've been able to get your enterprise off to a good start," Alec said with a smile.

That wasn't all that had gotten off to a good start. Mrs. Macdonald and his mother had become fast friends as soon as they'd met. It had been a huge relief to Alec, who wanted his future parents-in-law to get along well with his mother and soon-to-be stepfather. Yet, it didn't seem to have had much of an effect on the relationship between his mother and Anna. They were still walking on eggshells around each other, though to be fair, he and Anna had been treading a very delicate path for weeks themselves.

True to his word, Alec bathed quickly and dressed even faster. When he made his way back downstairs, his mother was wearing her wedding gown. She had chosen a simple blue silk dress without adornment. The color was traditional, and it looked good on her. Alec smiled. "You look lovely," he told her as he offered her his arm. "Shall we go and get you married?"

She nodded and beamed at him. He bent down and

pressed a kiss to her cheek, careful not to smudge her rouge or muss her carefully pinned hair. All the other women in the house said their goodbyes and hurried over to the saloon. "You are sure you don't mind that I'll be gone?" she teased him.

"As long as you drop a casserole by from time to time, I think I'll survive," he joked.

"I'm happy to come back if ever you need me."

"No, your husband needs you. If I need any help, I can hire someone to keep house for me. You have a new man to care for now, and his needs will be far more interesting for you than mine."

"You don't have any needs, that's why," his mother said as they stepped onto the porch together. "You're too good at looking after yourself."

Alec patted her hand where it lay on his arm. "You raised me well, Mama."

"What went wrong between you and Dr. Anna?" she asked him unexpectedly.

"I don't know what you mean," he said awkwardly. He didn't dare say that he'd felt he had been unable to choose Anna over her.

"You were inseparable. At least as inseparable as two people like the two of you can be. Both of you work too hard, too many hours." She shook her head. "But you suited each other because of that. Neither of you would ever have resented it in the other." She paused, turning to look him in the eye. "It was because of me, wasn't it? You feared I would interfere too much."

"No, Mama," Alec protested. But she was right, as she always was.

"Yes, Mama," she said with a sad smile. "I'm sorry, I never meant to get in your way. I should never have hidden those letters. I was so afraid you wouldn't have time for me if you found a bride. I feared an insipid little mouse that would keep house and raise babies and bore you silly."

"Anna is not insipid," Alec said, an image of her flashing into his mind. He knew she could tackle any crisis that came her way.

"No, she is not," his mother said dryly. "And I should have been kinder to her. But when you fear someone may steal away the person you love more than your own life, you do silly things. I will apologize to her, I promise. She was raised by dear Emmeline, so she can't be all bad."

It was quite a confession. Alec couldn't help wishing it had come three months earlier when everything had been good between himself and Anna. Now, everything felt as though it had fallen into place just a little too late. He took a deep breath. "We shall be late," he said, and he and his mother continued their procession along Main Street to the saloon.

He heard his mother gasp as they entered the back room. "Oh, you made it beautiful for us," she cried, a tear in her eye.

"I couldn't have your big day in something that actually

looked like the back of a saloon," Alec said, pleased to have surprised her and happy that she liked all he had done.

"You are a good boy. You've always been the very best of sons."

Everyone turned around as they entered, and a hushed silence ensued as they walked down the makeshift aisle toward Dr. Lancelot. The good doctor was still beaming from ear to ear and looked utterly delighted when Alec placed his mother's hand into his. Alec stood back, his eyes scanning the crowd of people for Anna's golden hair. He couldn't see her anywhere.

He barely heard a word of the ceremony because he was wondering what might have happened to her. She had said she would be there, and Anna never broke a promise. Perhaps there had been a medical emergency that she'd had to attend as Dr. Lancelot could hardly leave his own wedding. But as the ceremony ended and she was still not there, Alec couldn't help feeling that she'd decided not to come.

He couldn't blame her. He should have asked her to be his wife when they'd been in Chicago. He should have brought her to Iron Creek as his bride, not as he had done, as an acquaintance his mother needed to grow accustomed to. He should have done everything in his power to make her happy, to keep her by his side. But he'd put his mother first. He'd worried about her needs above anyone else's, including his own. And because of that, he was now the one left alone, not his mama.

Dr. Lancelot led his bride out of the wedding chamber and along the street to Iron Creek's new hotel, where Mr. and Mrs. Macdonald had laid on a splendid wedding breakfast for all their guests. Alec felt his heart lift when he saw Anna directing a group of the town's young people as they brought platters of food and drinks from the kitchens.

Of course she was there, and Alec castigated himself. Her mother had said as much back at the house. She'd probably just not had time to attend the ceremony because there was so much to do. Knowing her generosity, she had probably insisted her parents attend as her mother and his had become such close friends. Anna looked perfect, her golden hair a halo around her lovely face, and her dark blue dress accentuating the color of her beautiful eyes. He felt a pain in his belly when she glanced up, saw him, and immediately turned away.

He watched nervously as his mother approached her, then marveled as the two of them laughed together and shared a warm embrace as if they were long-lost friends finally reunited. His mother glanced his way for a moment, and Alec knew they were talking about him. But Anna did not look his way. She shook her head and seemed to make her excuses before disappearing back into the kitchens.

Mama began heading his way but paused when the sound of a spoon on glass interrupted everyone's conversations. Dr. Lancelot was standing at the end of the room, his sharp eyes scanning the space for his bride. "Ah, there you are, my dear," he said when his eyes rested upon her. "Would you care to join me as I thank our guests for being here with us today?"

She gave Alec a gentle look, then joined her husband. Dr. Lancelot gave an excellent speech, and everyone raised their glasses to toast the new couple. Alec didn't wait to hear the other speeches friends and neighbors gave as the town celebrated together. Instead, he made his way outside. The gardens had yet to be created, but there was a vast expanse of grass outside, littered with the remains of the construction work that had so recently been completed. Alec kicked at a lump of oak, then cursed as he stubbed his toe, having forgotten how solid wood could be.

"What did it ever do to you?" a familiar voice asked.

Alec turned around to see Anna, who had stepped outside for a moment, too. "It was simply there," he said.

"That hardly seems a good enough reason."

Alec stared at her. He had all the reason in the world to kick whatever he liked. He'd ruined everything with her and could not see how he might put any of it right. "What would be a good reason?" he asked.

"I don't know. Perhaps that you feel you've been a fool, that you've let something, someone, get away that you should have held onto so tightly that they might have been unable to breathe?" she said dispassionately.

"Is that what I've done?" he asked. "Did I let you get away? Is it too late to put it right?"

"I don't know," she said sadly. "I came here from Boston

with no idea of what to expect. I met you in Chicago, where everything seemed perfect. We saved Wilfred, we went to the theater and to the concert hall, to the park and the zoological gardens. We talked about everything. And you found me a position where there was none."

"We did, and I did," he agreed.

"I made the choice to follow my heart rather than my head. Copperton Mill was the wise choice, the one where there was no emotional nonsense on either side that might influence the outcome of its success or failure. But I chose to come here, to be with you, whatever that might bring." Her voice faltered a little as she spoke, and her eyes were filled with tears. Alec had never seen her look like that before. She was always so composed and so calm in every situation. Yet now, he couldn't be sure if she was sad or angry. Perhaps she was both.

He couldn't hide his surprise to hear her say such things. But he could see that she meant every word. "You've never said that before. If I'd known—"

"If you'd known?" she exploded. "What precisely would you have done differently if you'd known? And you had to have known. How could you not? I made no mystery of my feelings for you."

It was true enough. Even though they had both said the words, it seemed so long ago, and he hadn't fully let himself believe that they might be true, but her actions had certainly told him in no uncertain terms how much she cared for him. She had given up the opportunity to open her own practice in a town where there was no overbearing potential mother-in-law to scupper her happiness and come to Iron Creek, knowing that she would only ever be the junior partner in Dr. Lancelot's practice and that Alec's mother may never come around to even the idea of her.

"What more did I need to do, Alec?" she demanded.

"Nothing. You needed to do nothing. It was all me, my insecurities, and my need to be sure Mama would actually marry and leave the house," he blurted out, not caring that everything he'd hoped to say was not what he was saying. None of this had worked out the way he'd hoped. He'd lost her. He might as well let her know just what a fool he'd been so she would know that none of it was her fault. "She is the most loving, the most wonderful mother a boy could have. She lavished me with love, did everything for me. But when my father died she was broken into pieces. I knew I could never mend them, but I could at least give her a reason to keep going —caring for me. I couldn't take that away from her, and I was too afraid she would become like that once more."

"I know all that," Anna said patiently. "I understood all that. What I don't understand is why, once it was clear that she would be taken care of, you didn't come straight to me and ask for my hand? You didn't even talk to me about why you were hesitating. Did you not think I would fear it was something I had done?"

Alec pulled out the ring he had kept in his pocket since Dr. Lancelot had proposed to his mother. "I bought this the day they told me of their plans," he said. "I should have come to you then. I know that. But I was so afraid it would have been for nothing if anything went wrong."

"Did you not ever think that, eventually, your mother and I might come to some kind of truce?" Anna asked him.

"Honestly?" Alec asked. Anna nodded. "No, I thought my mother would resist until her dying day. She is that stubborn."

"And you are not?" Anna raised an eyebrow and gave him a sardonic smile.

"You are probably right, but you hold your own in the determination department yourself," he teased. She smiled, and Alec felt a weight lift from his shoulders. They were talking as they usually did. Something had shifted.

"Anna Macdonald…" he started. He paused when he felt a surge of butterflies fill his belly but continued when they all took off and flew away at once. "I have been a fool, and I am sorrier than you can ever know. But, if you can see past that and look kindly on me once again, I promise I will never do anything without talking to you about it first, and I will never let you down again. Will you please be my wife?"

EPILOGUE

July 1881, Iron Creek, Minnesota

The new church was full of smiling faces. Anna was positively beaming as she looked down at the child in her arms and wondered how such a thing could come about, something so very perfect in every way. Baby Thomas Harding and his sisters, May and Daisy, were all clad in long, lace baptism gowns and were being unusually quiet as they waited for their baptism to commence. Each child was in the arms of its godparent. Anna had been honored to have been asked to be a guide for Katy's son. Daisy cooed to herself and reached up toward Mrs. Havermeier's face. The kindly landlady had travelled from Chicago just to be here. She had been so sweet to both Anna and Katy and had been more than proud when she'd been asked to attend the baptism and act as Daisy's godmother. And Mary Jellicoe had been chosen for May. She gently jiggled the always energetic child and whispered sweet nothings to keep her calm.

It was not the first time, and it would certainly not be the last, that Anna gave thanks that the triplets had been born healthy and well. Poor Katy had not enjoyed the most pleasant of pregnancies, but Zaaga's skills and herbal tonics had helped her through it, and Zaaga and Anna had delivered the triplets on a snowy night in January to the delight and wonder of both their parents. She gently stroked her own flat belly and prayed that she would be so blessed before too long.

There were many Ojibwe there, too. They tended to crowd at the back of the church, just outside the door. They were curious enough to wish to be a part of Garrett's family's celebrations in Iron Creek but not entirely happy to take a full part in the proceedings. Anna knew, however, that there was no hesitancy at all at their own gatherings. The triplets had enjoyed their naming ceremony within days of their birth, and so now had their Ojibwe names and heritage to keep them linked to that world from the start of their young lives.

When it was her turn to speak during the ceremony, Anna spoke with the same clear voice she'd used to make her vows to Alec, though that ceremony had been held in the back of the saloon to please his mother. There had been word that a new church would be built at the opposite end of town, where the Catholics in the community would be able to worship, but

Anna, like her husband, didn't mind where she thanked God for his guidance.

Before long the rites were finished, and the triplets had been accepted into God's church and the community of Iron Creek. At a party that Anna's parents had offered to throw for the Hardings at the hotel, they were passed around from neighbor to neighbor. Anna took a moment to sit and think about how much had changed in less than two years. Back then, she could never have imagined that she would be living in Minnesota, married to the man she loved, and working as a doctor for people she cared deeply about. Everything had been so much more precarious.

She smiled as her parents hurried past with platters of food. If they had expected running a hotel to be easier than running a farm, they had been much mistaken. But though it was still hard work, they seemed to love it and had found a new lease on life in Iron Creek. They were happier than she had ever known them to be, and she loved having them so close by she could stop in for a cup of tea every day.

The town's medical practice was growing. She and Dr. Lancelot had taken on another doctor and a nurse. The rumor the railway line might stretch further out from Duluth up to Grand Marais and perhaps beyond had brought many more people to the town. Alec's mother had been briefly put out by the idea of new nurses, but she had soon been delighted when it meant she had more people to keep organized and on their toes now that she had taken over the running of not just Dr.

Lancelot's home but also the clinic. Nelly was delighted to be able to leave behind all the paperwork and get back to nursing.

Alec joined Anna on the terrace. "What are you thinking about?" he asked. He put an arm around her shoulders and kissed the top of her head. "You have that dreamy look on your face that you get when you are truly happy."

"I am thinking about everything that has happened in the past two years," Anna admitted to him. "It hasn't always been easy, has it? But it has turned out remarkably well."

Alec pulled her closer and kissed her lips tenderly. "I think so," he agreed. "I'm sorry I almost ruined everything."

"You don't need to keep apologizing," Anna said happily. "We worked it out, as I hope we always will."

"I love you, Mrs. Jenks," he said.

"And you are the only person who will ever call me that and live to tell the tale," Anna teased. To everyone in town, she was Dr. Anna, and she liked that. To fellow medics when she entered into correspondence with them, she was Dr. Jenks, and she liked that, too. But with Alec she was either just Anna or Mrs. Jenks—and she loved them both.

"I hope so," he said. He kissed her again.

"I have something to tell you," she said, biting her lip a little apprehensively. "I know that we are both busy with work and that we said we would wait a while, but it seems that God had other plans for us." She glanced down at her belly meaningfully.

Alec stared at her as she ran her hands over her belly.

Anna waited for the fog to lift. She could see it in his eyes when it did. They lit up so brightly, then he smiled. Finally, he flung his arms around her, picked her up, and whirled her around. "Careful," she cried.

He slowed down and set her back on her feet, patting a little awkwardly at her belly. "Of course, you're right. We must be careful. Don't want anything to happen to the little one before he's even had a chance to grow."

"*She's* well protected in there," Anna said with a laugh. "I was thinking that at that speed, I might be likely to be quite sick. I wanted to save your lovely suit."

He shook his head, unable to stop grinning. "I can't believe it," he said, pulling her close against his body. "How could a man be any happier?"

"You don't mind that it has happened so soon?" she asked.

"Not one bit. I must confess I've been rather hankering for one of my own since the triplets arrived. I just didn't want to push you too soon. I know how much your work means to you."

"And I will not be giving that up. I rather thought that a nanny might be an excellent idea. Someone to help me out so I can keep working once she's born."

"Did you have anyone in mind?"

"Well, in her recent letters to me, my old landlady has been saying how unhappy she is and how much she misses me. She raised three sons and has eleven grandchildren, though they are all almost grown now. I think she might like to have a little one to care for again."

"Then you must write and invite her. I should be delighted to meet the most esteemed Mrs. Phelps, and if you believe she is the best person to care for our child, I am sure you are right," Alec assured her.

"You should fetch your mother. We should tell her and my parents," Anna said to him. He kissed her unhurriedly and then did as she'd asked. He returned with his mother and Dr. Lancelot in no time. Anna's parents hurried past again, this time on their way back to the kitchen. Anna beckoned to them. "Mom, Dad, Mama, Andrew. We have some news."

Alec's mother nudged Anna's. "I told you so," she said. "She's been filling out for weeks now. I saw the signs."

"You really should wait to be sure that is their news," Dr. Lancelot said to his wife with an indulgent smile.

"But I'm right, aren't I?" she demanded.

"Yes, you're right," Alec said. He hugged her tightly and kissed her on the forehead.

"And we are delighted," Anna's mom said, clasping her hands together tightly and beaming.

"Congratulations to you both," Anna's dad said. He gave his daughter a hug, then Dr. Lancelot embraced her and kissed her cheek.

"I don't have to find another doctor now, do I?" he asked her.

"Of course, you don't," Alec's mother exclaimed. "Anna

doesn't need to give up her work, does she? She's perfectly capable of being both mother and doctor, aren't you, my dear?"

Everyone laughed out loud. "Oh, Mama," Alec said. "How far you've come!"

The End

OTHER SERIES BY KARLA

Sun River Brides

Ruby Springs Brides

Silver River Brides

Eagle Creek Brides

Iron Creek Brides

CONNECT WITH KARLA GRACEY

Visit my website at www.karlagracey.com to sign up to my newsletter and get free books and be notified as to when my new releases are available.

Made in the USA
Coppell, TX
23 December 2024

43403888R00125